Dear Reader,

As head of cardiology at Yale-New Haven, I've made a number of discoveries regarding the heart, but it wasn't until Heather Cole walked into my life that I realized how much more there was to learn.

From the moment I saw her, my pulse started to race, my breath became rough and heavy, my heart began to throb until I thought it would burst. The symptoms couldn't be ignored.

She was the cause, and I knew the cure. I had to brush up on my bedside manner and go into private practice.

Robert McCrae, M.D.

1. ALABAMA
Full House • Jackie Weger
2. ALASKA
Borrowed Dreams • Debbie Macomber
3. ARIZONA
Call It Destiny • Jayne Ann Krentz
4. ARKANSAS
Another Kind of Love • Mary Lynn Baxter
5. CALIFORNIA
Deceptions • Annette Broadrick
6. COLORADO
Stormwalker • Dallas Schulze
7. CONNECTICUT
Straight from the Heart • Barbara Delinsky
8. DELAWARE
Author's Choice • Elizabeth August
9. FLORIDA
Dream Come True • Ann Major
10. GEORGIA
Way of the Willow • Linda Shaw
11. HAWAII
Tangled Lies • Anne Stuart
12. IDAHO
Rogue's Valley • Kathleen Creighton
13. ILLINOIS
Love by Proxy • Diana Palmer
14. INDIANA
Possibles • Lass Small
15. IOWA
Kiss Yesterday Goodbye • Leigh Michaels
16. KANSAS
A Time To Keep • Curtiss Ann Matlock
17. KENTUCKY
One Pale, Fawn Glove • Linda Shaw
18. LOUISIANA
Bayou Midnight • Emilie Richards
19. MAINE
Rocky Road • Anne Stuart
20. MARYLAND
The Love Thing • Dixie Browning
21. MASSACHUSETTS
Pros and Cons • Bethany Campbell
22. MICHIGAN
To Tame a Wolf • Anne McAllister
23. MINNESOTA
Winter Lady • Janet Joyce
24. MISSISSIPPI
After the Storm • Rebecca Flanders
25. MISSOURI
Choices • Annette Broadrick

26. MONTANA
Part of the Bargain • Linda Lael Miller
27. NEBRASKA
Secrets of Tyrone • Regan Forest
28. NEVADA
Nobody's Baby • Barbara Bretton
29. NEW HAMPSHIRE
Natural Attraction • Marisa Carroll
30. NEW JERSEY
Moments Harsh, Moments Gentle • Joan Hohl
31. NEW MEXICO
Within Reach • Marilyn Pappano
32. NEW YORK
In Good Faith • Judith McWilliams
33. NORTH CAROLINA
The Security Man • Dixie Browning
34. NORTH DAKOTA
A Class Act • Kathleen Eagle
35. OHIO
Too Near the Fire • Lindsay McKenna
36. OKLAHOMA
A Time and a Season • Curtiss Ann Matlock
37. OREGON
Uneasy Alliance • Jayne Ann Krentz
38. PENNSYLVANIA
The Wrong Man • Ann Major
39. RHODE ISLAND
The Bargain • Patricia Coughlin
40. SOUTH CAROLINA
The Last Frontier • Rebecca Flanders
41. SOUTH DAKOTA
For Old Times' Sake • Kathleen Eagle
42. TENNESSEE
To Love a Dreamer • Ruth Langan
43. TEXAS
For the Love of Mike • Candace Schuler
44. UTAH
To Tame the Hunter • Stephanie James
45. VERMONT
Finders Keepers • Carla Neggers
46. VIRGINIA
The Devlin Dare • Cathy Gillen Thacker
47. WASHINGTON
The Waiting Game • Jayne Ann Krentz
48. WEST VIRGINIA
All in the Family • Heather Graham Pozzessere
49. WISCONSIN
Starstruck • Anne McAllister
50. WYOMING
Special Touches • Sharon Brondos

BARBARA DELINSKY
Straight from the Heart

Connecticut

Harlequin Books

TORONTO • NEW YORK • LONDON
AMSTERDAM • PARIS • SYDNEY • HAMBURG
STOCKHOLM • ATHENS • TOKYO • MILAN
MADRID • WARSAW • BUDAPEST • AUCKLAND

HARLEQUIN ENTERPRISES LTD.
225 Duncan Mill Road, Don Mills,
Ontario, Canada M3B 3K9

STRAIGHT FROM THE HEART

Copyright © 1986 by Barbara Delinsky

All rights reserved. Except for use in any review, the reproduction
or utilization of this work in whole or in part in any form by any
electronic, mechanical or other means, now known or hereafter
invented, including xerography, photocopying and recording, or in
any information storage or retrieval system, is forbidden without
the permission of the publisher, Harlequin Enterprises Ltd.,
225 Duncan Mill Road, Don Mills, Ontario, Canada M3B 3K9

ISBN: 0-373-45157-1

Published Harlequin Enterprises, Ltd. 1986, 1993

All the characters in this book have no existence outside the
imagination of the author and have no relation whatsoever to
anyone bearing the same name or names. They are not even
distantly inspired by any individual known or unknown to the
author, and all incidents are pure invention.

® and ™ are trademarks used under license. Trademarks recorded
with ® are registered in the United States Patent and Trademark
Office, the Canadian Trade Marks Office and in other countries.

Printed in the U.S.A.

HEATHER COLE was an outsider trying to look as though she belonged. She kept her shoulders straight, her eyes level, her gait relaxed. When the few people dotting nearby paper-strewn tables paid her no heed, she slipped through the door into the large conference hall and, relieved that she'd been able to gain entrance without identification or commitment, found an unobtrusive resting spot against the rear wall.

Every seat was filled—not that she really wanted to sit. She wasn't sure if she wanted to be there at all, but something inside had pushed her. She had shopping to do in New Haven anyway, she reasoned, and the medical center was close to her escape route, the expressway.

A man stood at the podium, addressing the gathering of visiting medical personnel in a low monotone. Heather scanned the faces of the four men and women seated in an arc behind him, all specialists in one aspect of heart disease or another, so the bulletin she'd received had said. She wondered which one was Robert McCrae. In her mind, she'd formed an image of a distinguished-looking gentleman in his fifties, perhaps balding, very definitely a father figure. None of the faces she saw fit the image.

Polite applause interrupted Heather's speculation, and one of the female speakers rose from her chair and approached the podium. When she began to discuss arterial disease, Heather, who'd read and reread the agenda so many times that its contents were committed to memory, identified her as Elizabeth Palcomb. So the other woman, due to speak on arrhythmia, was Rita Connolly. And of the two men—which one was Robert McCrae?

Twenty minutes later she had her answer. The moderator returned to the podium and, with a minimum of words, introduced the doctor Heather had come to hear. Again there was applause. Heather stood straighter, her eye riveted to the man who approached the dais.

He was extremely tall, extremely well built, extremely good-looking. If he'd reached forty, she would have been surprised. Though there was a sternness about him—a hardness along his jaw, across the bridge of his nose—there was also an approachability. Perhaps, she mused, it was the relaxed set of his shoulders. Or the way his thick dark hair persisted, in spite of the hand he dashed across it, in falling over his brow.

His voice was deep and filled with confidence. "The treatment of heart valve disease has advanced dramatically in the past twenty years," he began, and for an instant Heather debated turning and running. Did she really want to hear this? She'd been doing fine, just fine for the past twenty years. Perhaps she was asking for trouble.

But she stayed in place, mesmerized as much by Robert McCrae's optimistic tone as by the dreamlike images that flitted through her mind. A husband—children—her running free across a meadow in the bright sunshine, breathless from happiness alone. How much she wanted those things that others so often took for granted!

She listened, entranced, barely moving during the fifteen-minute address. When Robert McCrae returned to his seat, her gaze lingered on him. Even seated, without a hospital coat or a stethoscope or a bevy of interns and residents by his side, he radiated capability. Intuitively she knew she'd trust him, but still she was frightened.

What frightened her most was that her future was in her own hands now. Her parents were dead. Their family doctor had shifted his practice to Florida, and Heather had neither rapport with nor faith in his replacement. And since she rarely mentioned her physical condition to friends or acquaintances, she couldn't look to them for encouragement one way or another. She was alone, and the responsibility for her action—or inaction—weighed heavily on her mind.

Anxious to relieve the burden as she'd always done, by blocking it out and concentrating on brighter things, Heather slipped out into the hall. She would fetch her car and drive home, she decided. It had been a long day. Wanting to avoid the worst of the crowd, she'd been at the stores when they'd first opened. She'd secured a bundle of fantastic pieces of suede, a bagful of magnificent silk needlework threads and a boxful of tiny, vividly colored beads, as well as interfacing, a fresh supply of needles and thread and a bolt of canvas. New materials always gave her a lift, and she'd be heading home with a loaded car. Thus fortified, she was set to attack the order her buyer had phoned in the week before.

Heather glanced back at the doors now closed behind her and felt a faint nagging.

She was hungry. That was it. She'd get a bite to eat before leaving the medical center.

Following the simple directions given her at a nearby information booth, she found the coffee shop and sat down to a carton of yogurt, some rye crackers and a cup of weak tea. Ignoring the hospital personnel and visitors around her, she firmly directed her thoughts back to Chester, her haven, and her work.

She had much to be grateful for. Her home was a delight. It was old but charming, and had responded well to the renovation she'd commissioned. Quiet and serene, it was the perfect place to work, which she did with pleasure.

She smiled at the thought of how her business had mushroomed. From that first set of handbags given out on consignment six years ago had grown standing orders from some of the finest stores and boutiques up and down the East Coast. She'd been urged to expand, to take on help and double her volume, but she'd resisted, convinced that the very scarcity of her bags was an integral part of their appeal.

She'd been fortunate. Luck had been with her, and timing. The buyers insisted that her success was due to skill and dedication, but she was too modest to wholeheartedly agree. She loved what she did, which made dedication a breeze, and as for skill, well, she knew there were many craftsmen more talented than she who simply didn't have an eye for the market as she did. And it was no wonder! She'd daydreamed over high-fashion magazines for years, so a feel for style was second nature to her. And now that she'd made her mark in the field, she was privy to inside information as to what shapes and colors and textures designers would be promoting six months to a year down the road.

Draining the last of her tea, she gathered her empty cups and papers together and deposited them in a nearby receptacle. Assuring herself that she didn't want to get lost, she returned the way she'd come, passing the conference room just as the doors opened and the attendants began to stream out.

Her step slowed. Twosomes and threesomes passed her, many in lab coats or white uniforms, others in street clothes. She cast a glance over her shoulder and saw that Rita Connolly, of arrhythmia renown, was talking with a cluster of people.

Heather told herself to keep walking, but her feet didn't obey. She found herself stopping by a full-length window, turning, putting both hands against the wood guardrail by her hips. She looked at the conference room door, then away. Curiosity. That was all it was. But when Dr. Robert McCrae emerged to stand in the corridor in deep conversation with two of the conference attendees, Heather knew it wasn't simple curiosity making her heart pound.

She had a problem. Robert McCrae could well have the solution. But did she want ... could she ... what if there was a complication, or if things were worse than she thought?

For some reason he glanced her way. She quickly looked down. Again she told herself to move. Again her body disobeyed. She shifted her gaze to the window, but within minutes she was looking back at the doctor.

He was even taller than he'd appeared to be behind the podium. More broad shouldered. Stronger-looking. He seemed intent as he talked and the sternness was there, but he was still very animated, and when he smiled, which he did once, she could see faint grooves in his cheeks.

His gaze skittered over the milling group, catching hers a second time. A second time she looked away. When she finally dared seek him out again, new people had joined him. He was listening closely, his head bent, his brow furrowed, not in worry but in concentration. With one hand buried in the pocket of his gray slacks, his navy blazer was pushed back to reveal a crisp white shirt, a solid chest, a lean, belted waist.

Heather couldn't help but stare. She tried to picture the man in operating room garb, with a gauze mask covering his mouth and nose, but even the small shudder of apprehension the image caused wasn't enough to make her look away.

She shouldn't have come. One part of her screamed it. The other part, though, held her rooted to the spot, and she felt herself torn in two directions at once. She should leave; she should stay. She should ignore her problem; she should attend to it.

Wistfully she looked at the stragglers now retreating down the corridor. Dismally she looked back at Robert McCrae. Their eyes met and held. It wasn't too late, she realized, her heart thudding softly against her breast. No one knew she was here. No one would have to know. She'd simply leave before anything happened and forget that she'd ever come.

Robert McCrae knew the instant she straightened from the guardrail. He'd originally thought she was waiting for someone, but then he'd caught the nervous way she was looking at him. Looking, looking away, looking again. He'd seen her inside the conference room, standing against the back wall, leaving soon after he'd finished speaking. He didn't know what had brought her to the medical center, but instinct told him that her reasons were as important as those of the rest of the audience, if not more so.

At the risk of offending those who'd remained to talk with him, he excused himself with a brief apology and headed down the corridor. Damn but she was moving fast, he thought, as though she were fleeing someone or something. When she rounded a corner and he lost sight of her, he broke into a jog, catching up only after she'd left the building and was making her way down the front steps.

"Hey, hold up!" He lightly clasped her arm.

Startled, Heather swung her head around. Her shoulder-length hair echoed the movement, swirling against her cheeks before settling. Unfortunately it was the only thing that did settle. Her eyes widened; her pulse raced; her stomach curled into a knot. Her escape had been thwarted by none other than the man who'd inspired it. Only with a great effort did she maintain an outer semblance of composure.

Sensing her inner tension, Robert gentled his voice. "I saw you in the conference room. Up in back. Then again in the corridor just now. Were you waiting to see me?"

"No," she answered too quickly, then bit her lip. Her voice was higher than usual, but never having heard her speak, the doctor didn't know that, she reasoned. Of course, she had no idea that guilt was written all over her face.

Robert couldn't miss it. He chanced a small smile. "That's too bad. I was really in need of an escape from the group back there." His hand hadn't left her arm, and very subtly he urged her into step alongside him. "Where are you headed?"

"I, uh, I'm on my way home," she managed, unable to take her eyes from his. They were gray and intent, not at all distracted as she might have thought such a busy doctor's would be. She thought of the approachability she'd sensed in him from the first, and she wondered if he was that way with patients.

"Have time for a cup of coffee?" he asked. He knew that there was something on her mind, also knew that it would take some coaxing to get it out. A casual coffee break was a possible vehicle.

"I really can't," Heather answered breathlessly. "I'd like to get home before the traffic mounts up."

"Where's home?"

She hesitated for just an instant before deciding that no harm could come from giving such a simple piece of information. "Chester."

He digested that as they continued to walk. Chester was in the Connecticut Valley, a small town, quaint, picturesque and distinctly colonial. It seemed fitting that the young woman beside him should be from there. Chester was as unspoiled as she appeared to be. Not that unspoiled meant unpolished; though simple in design, her linen suit was chic and sophisticated. "Do you come to the city often?"

"Only when I need supplies."

"Supplies?"

"I make handbags." Another harmless fact, she reasoned.

He nodded, wanting to know more but feeling the urgency of one other question. "What brought you to the medical center?"

If Heather could have run then, she would have. But there was the matter of Robert McCrae's fingers still circling her arm...and the tacit admission of guilt a speedy escape would surely constitute. With due effort, she gathered her senses and forced herself to calm down.

"I received a bulletin announcing today's lectures. They sounded interesting, and since I was in the neighborhood..."

Robert was tempted to remind her that she'd left soon after he'd finished speaking and that, though she claimed to be wary of traffic, she'd hung around the corridor until the rest of the lectures were done. But he knew better than to put her on the spot. She seemed skittish, unsure, worried, if the way she gnawed on her lower lip was any indication.

"The audience consisted primarily of personnel from neighboring hospitals and medical centers," he ventured. "I'm afraid we didn't expect many laymen to attend. Not that I object, mind you. Outreach is one of the major goals of hospital publications, and lectures such as today's are usually open. You must be on our mailing list."

She didn't look at him, but she couldn't have said where they were walking, either. He was simply guiding her, slowly, comfortably. And strangely, she trusted him not to lead her astray. "I donate money now and again. In turn I get periodic newsletters."

"And you read them. That's more than most do."

She looked up at him in surprise. "I *always* read them." Indeed, there were certain articles she'd read and reread, then tucked in the back of her mind, suppressed but never quite forgotten. "Medicine is a fascinating field. There are new diagnostic techniques, new methods of treatment, new theories of prevention."

"Particularly in the field of cardiac care," he injected meaningfully. "We're living at a time of great optimism. That's one of the things I was trying to say today. . . . Did it get across?"

Heather swallowed. There was optimism and there was optimism. It was one thing to hear talk of statistics, even specific case studies. It was quite another to put oneself in the position of possibly being among the failures.

"I think so," she said, wishing she sounded more sure of herself, if for his sake alone. He was a good doctor, a *superior* doctor, if the press reports she'd read about him were correct. And they had to be. Gazing up at him now, realizing again how relatively young he was, she knew that to be the chief of cardiology at as prestigious a teaching hospital as the Yale-New Haven he had to be *outstanding*.

"Such conviction," he chided with a dry chuckle, then looked ahead and nodded to a passing colleague.

Only then did Heather check out her surroundings. Robert McCrae was leading her up the steps toward another building. "Uh, I really have to run," she exclaimed nervously. Though she held back, she didn't quite pull away.

"Twenty minutes. That's all I ask." This time his chuckle was a rueful one. "That's all I have, actually. I've got an afternoon packed with appointments, but it's been a long time since breakfast and I could use a little something. Keep me company. Please?"

"But you'll want to be talking with other doctors—"

"I talk with other doctors all the time. It's not everyday that I get a chance to talk with a craftswoman."

"But I really don't have much to say—"

"Let me be the judge of that," he interrupted again, putting his hand lightly at the back of her waist and drawing her onward.

Heather didn't argue further. For one thing, she didn't want to make a scene. For another, surprisingly, she didn't want to leave. Not yet, at least. Now that she'd gotten over the initial shock of a face-to-face confrontation with Robert McCrae, she was aware of feeling oddly relaxed with him. Safe.

Before long they were winding through a small cafeteria. Robert nodded in greeting to various people they passed, but he steered her to a quiet corner table set apart from the rest.

"Are you sure this is all you'll have?" he asked, removing an apple from his tray and holding it out to her.

She smiled sheepishly. "I had yogurt and crackers after I left the conference hall. This is dessert."

So she'd gone to the coffee shop and then returned, he mused. There was definitely something on her mind. Pondering what it might be, he removed a turkey sandwich from the tray, then a carton of milk, a container of pudding and a cup of steaming coffee. "None of this even?" he asked, pointing to the coffee as he set the tray aside.

"I don't drink coffee. Too much caffeine."

He folded his long frame into the seat opposite her. "Wise lady. Yogurt, an apple, no caffeine—I wish half of my patients were as conscientious as you. I wish *I* were as conscientious as you." His lips thinned resignedly. "Unfortunately I need all the stimulation I can get. It's been a long day already and it's far from over."

"What time do you start?"

"In the morning? I'm usually here by six."

"And you finish up . . . ?"

"Somewhere between seven and eight at night."

Heather's eyes grew round in appreciation. "That's a full day."

He stuck a straw in the carton of milk and took a long sip before answering. "And a busy one. More often than not I wish the day were even longer. I never seem to get as much done as I want. Long after my body's shut down for the day, my mind keeps going."

"It must be very rewarding, what you do."

"It is." He removed the plastic wrapper from his sandwich. "Demanding and challenging, heartbreaking at times, but, yes, rewarding."

She felt a frisson of unease. "Heartbreaking—you mean when a patient doesn't make it?"

Robert noted the shadow that passed over her features and took a more positive tack. "Yes. But I like to think of those who do, of those who wouldn't have had a chance if they hadn't come to us. It's truly miraculous what we're able to do nowadays. What with the heart-lung machine, vastly improved instruments and methods and man-made materials, we can do unbelievable repair jobs." He stopped, took a bite of his sandwich and waited, hoping that she'd broach the subject of whatever it was that had brought her to the medical center. When she simply munched on her apple, he took the bull by the horns.

"Usually lay people who attend lectures such as today's have specific reasons for doing so, most often a sick friend or relative. They're doing research, so to speak, intending to pass on the information they hear. Is that the case with you?"

She swallowed a chunk of apple whole and had to clear her throat before speaking. "No."

"No father with a heart condition, or sister, or cousin?" She shook her head. "I was just curious."

He narrowed his gaze in mock suspicion. "Then you're a journalist."

"I told you." Her heart was pumping faster. "I make handbags."

He let her off the hook for the moment, dropping his gaze to the bag that hung from two leather braids by her chair. "Did you make that one?"

"Yes."

"May I see it?"

She raised the rectangular, intricately pieced leather bag and passed it across the table, then sat back somewhat apprehensively while Robert McCrae studied it. There was good reason why she'd never marketed her bags herself. Each one was dear to her heart, its creation something akin, she imagined, to giving birth. She didn't think she could bear watching someone lift it, turn it, poke at it and then put it down in dismissal and turn away.

Robert McCrae didn't put it down in dismissal, or turn away. "This is remarkable," he exclaimed in a deep voice. "Did you do it all yourself?"

His approval brought a quick smile to her face. "Uh-huh."

He dragged his gaze from her smile and traced the fine needlework on the front of the bag. "Even this?"

"Uh-huh."

"You're very talented." He turned the bag again. "Are your others like this?"

"I use different patterns and materials and colors. Some are woven, some made of carpet. Some have beading instead of needlepoint. But I suppose you could say that all my bags have a . . . distinctive look to them."

"I'll say—not that I'm an expert on handbags. Where do you sell them?"

She named several boutiques in New York City. "Neiman-Marcus and Bloomingdale's carry them, too, but on a limited basis. I can only make so many a week."

"How many?"

"Twenty."

He looked at the bag a final time before returning it to her. "Unbelievable. It must keep you busy. You have assistants, don't you?"

"Nope. Just me."

"And you make twenty bags like this in a week? I'd think the handwork on one alone would take days."

"It's not so bad, actually. The basic patterns for a week's work are similar, so I cut and stitch all the fabric first. The handwork is the fun part. I sit back in a comfortable chair, listen to music and work away. It's very relaxing." And tailor-made for her. Minimal physical exertion, minimal psychological stress.

"Sounds it." But he was homing in on what she hadn't said. "Then you don't have a family? A husband?"

After a split second's hesitation, she murmured, "No."

He heard the hesitation, caught the ghost of a crease between her eyes before it disappeared, and sensed he was getting warmer. "I'm surprised."

"Surprised? Why?"

He took another bite of his sandwich, then shrugged. "I don't know. Aside from the matter of volume, your work would fit beautifully around kids. You seem very nurturing." Soft was the word he wanted to use, but it sounded too suggestive. "You're the right age. You're attractive and successful."

Heather had averted her gaze and was skimming the rest of the cafeteria, seeing nothing. She *wanted* a husband and kids. And yes, she knew that her work could easily accommodate them. But that was only part of her present discomfort. That Dr. Robert McCrae should be calling her attractive and successful was unsettling. She attempted to steer the conversation elsewhere, but underestimated the perverse tenacity of the wayward part of her.

"How about you? Your work sounds a little less yielding than mine. It must be hard on your family."

"I'm divorced," he said without pause. "You're right. My work is far less yielding. That's pretty much what broke the marriage up."

Though he didn't seem in any pain, she felt instantly contrite. "I'm sorry. I shouldn't have asked."

Robert tried to stifle a smile. "Why not? I started it." She was soft *and* sensitive.

At a loss for words, Heather simply sent him a helpless look. He found it to be soft, sensitive *and* honest, and before he knew it he was making a confession. "Anyway, it's okay. My ex-wife was right when she accused me of being unfaithful. My work is my mistress, and I've never wanted it otherwise. Gail and I have been divorced for seven years. She's remarried and is much happier now. I can accept that." He paused and frowned. "What's harder to accept is that I have two children I barely know."

Heather's eyes widened. "Two children?" she breathed, more than a little envious.

"Michael is ten, Dawn is twelve. They were very young—three and five—when we split, and I was just as bad a father as a husband during the years we were together."

Drawn into his story, Heather momentarily forgot where she was and whom she was with. "Do you see them often?"

Robert shook his head. His frown faded, leaving a gentle sadness. "Gail has custody. They live in San Francisco—that's where I was working when we were together, and her present husband has always lived there—but the grandparents are all on this coast. I see the kids when they come visiting on holidays and vacations." He nudged the remains of his sandwich around his plate and took a deep breath. "I suppose I could see them more. Gail wouldn't object. But the fact of the matter is that I don't know what to do with them. They're as awkward around me as I am around them." He raised his eyes to Heather's. "Sad, isn't it?"

"Yes," she said softly, without condemnation, "but mostly because you seem bothered by it. Your mistress falls short, evidently."

"No, not really. In my day-to-day life I'm not aware of lacking anything. It's just when I think of Michael and Dawn that I feel badly." Head tucked low, he ran a finger along the side of his nose. When he glanced up at Heather from beneath his brows, his cheeks were flushed. "I don't know why I'm telling you this. I don't usually bore people with my personal life." More aptly, he usually maintained a professional distance. He still didn't know why this woman was at the hospital.

"There's nothing at all boring about your life," Heather protested, her eyes growing brighter. "You have a wonderful job and an unbelievable reputation. You travel—"

"How do you know that?"

"Past newsletters. And you write—I've seen your books. You've been married. You have children." She shook her head in amazement. "Compared to someone like me, you've done so much *living*. In spite of the situation with your kids, I'm green with envy."

His expression softened. "You don't look green. Maybe a little pale. Too much work and too little play. What *do* you do for play?"

His comment about her color and the question that followed it toppled Heather back to earth. "For play?" she echoed meekly, her gaze dropping to the apple core she turned in her fingers. "Oh, I read...or shop...or take walks in the country." Actually, the walks were most frequently around her backyard, which was country aplenty. And though the sedate pace of them didn't bother her, the fact that she was more often than not alone did.

As though he'd read her mind, Robert tilted his head. "Have you a steady date, or a fiancé?"

"No."

"No special man?"

"No."

That surprised him even more than her being single; people had wised up since his time and were marrying later and later. But she was so lovely, with her dark, shiny hair, her delicate features, her soft voice and her wealth of compassion, that he couldn't imagine any man being oblivious to her charm. Of course, there was always the possibility, he reminded himself, that the offers were there but she turned them down.

"Do your parents live nearby?" he asked, unable to believe she was totally alone.

"They're both dead."

"Then you must have friends in Chester."

She looked up with a tremulous smile. "Oh, yes. The people there are wonderful. Very caring." But it wasn't the same. Whereas her neighbors and the others she called friends were warm and generous and protective in their way, they weren't family. The element of love was missing.

Robert read between the lines, cued by a clipped phrase here, a suspended tone there. "Are you lonely?" he asked quietly.

She tried to force a laugh, but it sounded slightly wooden. "Aren't we all at times?"

"I suppose. Let me rephrase that, then. Do you *want* a family?"

She nodded solemnly. "I'd like that more than anything, I think. It's not that I'm unhappy now. I've been fortunate in so many things, and I don't mean to sound ungrateful. But a family would be nice. I dream about it sometimes...."

Her words trailed off as she suddenly realized the extent of her disclosure. She'd never been one to confide in strangers, and though she'd known about Dr. Robert McCrae for months, he was personally still a stranger. Yet he had a way about him—perhaps it was bedside manner—that generated confidence. She was sure that what she'd told him would remain between the two of them, but... Had she told him too much, or not enough? It would be so easy to blurt out the rest now, to tell him that she suffered from valve stenosis, that she'd come to hear him speak with an ear toward seeing if he could help her, that she'd been told she should have surgery before she ventured to have children.

But then he'd know, and he'd urge her toward surgery, and she wasn't sure if she liked that idea. Besides, he was so strong and healthy that one part of her didn't want him to know of her weakness.

Jerkily she glanced down at her watch. "I've kept you too long. You'll be late for your appointments."

Robert had completely forgotten the time, a rarity for him. But, then, he reasoned as he reluctantly consulted his own watch, this woman was a rarity, too. There was something about her.... But she was on her feet, slinging the braided leather straps of her bag over her shoulder.

"Thank you for the apple, and for your time," she murmured hurriedly. "Good luck with your work—"

"Wait!" He gently grasped her wrist when she began to move off. "I, uh, will I see you again?"

"I don't know. Maybe someday... when I'm in town. . . ." She had to leave. Now! Those gray eyes of his were more intent than ever, and the urgency she felt had little to do with her medical condition. He was attractive, companionable, charming. It wouldn't do for her to develop a crush on her doctor even before she sought him out as such!

"But when will that be?" Robert asked. He was on his feet as well, unfortunately looking at her back as she hurried away. "I—wait!"

He was too late, and there were any number of curious eyes watching him. With great dignity, he sat back down in his chair and forced himself to eat his pudding. He knew he was running behind schedule, but he needed to understand what had just happened.

He'd met a woman, a lovely young woman, who had evoked his curiosity as no other had in fifteen years. She was quiet. Yes, she'd had her moments of nervousness, but there had been something serene about her. She was alone in the world, and vulnerable, he'd guess. And he didn't buy the reasons she'd given him for coming to the medical center, so there was that little bit of a challenge, of mystery about her.

Would he see her again? That was in her hands. Hell, he didn't even know her name!

THAT FACT bothered him most as the next weeks passed. He was as busy was ever, putting in fourteen-hour days at the hospital and then working at home, reviewing cases, charting treatment plans, weighing the pros and cons of recommending surgery for one patient or another. He flew to North Carolina to deliver a seminar at Duke, and returned, as always, to a backlog. But he didn't mind. He loved his work. Still, in the wee hours between work and sleep, or at odd times during meals or the commute to his Woodbridge home, he'd think of her and curse himself for not having gotten her name.

After two weeks had passed, he nonchalantly questioned his secretary.

"Helen, you haven't by chance received a call from a woman in Chester, have you?"

Helen O'Grady had been with him since he'd come to Yale six years before. She was in her late fifties, soft-spoken and competent, a widow with three grown children. If she tended to treat him on occasion like one of her children—reminding him to get lunch or a haircut or a good night's rest—he indulged her. She was sweet, kind in her pampering, and he rather liked it.

"Not that I know of," she answered cautiously. "What's her name?"

He feigned interest in the letters she'd just handed him to sign. "I don't know. I only know she's from Chester."

"Is she a referral?"

"No."

"A doctor?"

"Uh-uh."

Helen nodded once and Robert suddenly wished he'd said nothing. He didn't like the way she was looking at him. "She's just someone I ran into at a lecture several weeks ago," he murmured with a shrug, annoyed that he felt he had to offer an explanation. Turning, he headed for his office. "If she calls, let me know."

He was behind his desk before Helen could do more than nod again, and he quickly immersed himself in paperwork. Later that night, though, when he was lying in bed, he thought again about the nameless woman. From the first he'd sensed that there was something on her mind. He'd shanghaied her into having lunch—or an apple, as it turned out—so that he might put her at ease and, in so doing, free her from whatever fear it was that kept her mission a secret.

He'd failed. She'd fled from him cloaked in the same apprehension that had surrounded her when she'd stood nervously in the hall outside the conference room. Circumstance had dictated that his initial interest in her be professional, but as the few minutes they'd spent together grew more and more remote in time, what lingered in his mind was far removed from medicine.

He was intrigued that whoever-she-was had aroused his personal interest. If for no other reason, he wanted to see her again to decide if her elusiveness was the sole basis of his fascination.

So, one week later, he again broached the topic with Helen. He was careful to precede the question with several medical ones, to sound appropriately formal and businesslike.

"No call from Chester." He made it more a statement than a question. It wouldn't do to have Helen think he was waiting expectantly for the call.

"From Chester?" She hesitated for a minute, just long enough for him to betray himself by raising hopeful eyes. "Not yet.... Is she someone special?"

"How can I know that if I don't even know her name?" he asked gruffly, thinking that Helen O'Grady saw far too much.

"Very easily," Helen answered.

He glared at her. "And just what is that grin supposed to mean?"

If anything, the grin broadened, but she simply shrugged.

"Come on, Helen. Something's going on here. I'd like to know what it is."

"So would I."

Robert rolled his eyes. "Okay." He sighed. "Tell me what you're thinking...in as many words as you want." It was a joke between them. Ever efficient, Helen never wasted Robert's time with unnecessary conversation. If she had a message to give, she gave it succinctly. If she had a question to ask, she was direct and to the point. Only with Robert's permission did she give free reign to her tongue.

And he'd given permission now. "I've been working with you for six years now, Dr. McCrae, and I can decipher your moods nearly as easily as your handwriting. Even before you say a word I can tell when you've had a run-in with a cocky intern, when you've won a round with the men in the boardroom, when you've lost a patient." She cocked her head. "This time the look's new—at least for you. And it's about time."

"Whaddya mean, 'it's about time'?" Robert drawled, more curious now than angry. Though he'd never taken it to heart, he'd been aware of hospital gossip. He was alternately thought of as the "man of steel," the "granite fortress," or the "Hippocratic monk."

Helen sent him a chiding look. "Six years, and this is the very first time you've shown any sign of interest in a woman."

"Sign of interest? I simply asked if she'd called!"

"Twice now you've asked, each time trying to look as though you couldn't care less, but I know you." Her voice lowered in soft urging. "You really should date, Rob. You work far too hard."

"But I love my work."

"Sure you do. But your work is a possessive lover. Don't you think there's more to life? I've seen you leaving here headed for cocktail receptions honoring a trustee or a major donor, and I can't help but think how nice it would be if you had a woman on your arm, a woman to lead you away after an hour and take your mind off the hospital."

"You've been watching *General Hospital* on the sly," he teased, and drew an imaginary bow across an imaginary violin.

Helen smiled, but sadly this time. "You're wasting it, you know, all that youth and energy. And don't tell me that the hospital benefits from it, because there's so much in you that you could easily divert a little to your personal life and the hospital would never even notice."

Lips quirking on the fringe of a smile, Robert arched a brow. "Is that all, Mother?"

Silence resettled over her as she studied him a minute longer. Then she dropped her gaze to his tie and stared with such intensity that Robert glanced down.

"Oh-oh," he murmured, curving the tie up to examine it. "I did it again." Spattered antiseptic. Another trip to the dry cleaners. Shaking his head in dismay, he retreated to his office, deferring the rest of the official questions he had for Helen.

ANOTHER WEEK PASSED and there was no call from Chester. Robert began to ask himself why he was waiting. She hadn't said she'd call. She hadn't said she'd see him again.

Maybe. That was the word she'd used. It wasn't good enough for him.

He knew two basic facts about her: she lived alone in Chester and she made handbags. Briefly he contemplated driving to Chester and asking around. It was a small town. Chances were good that someone would know about the lady who sold handbags to Neiman-Marcus.

But he hated to do that. It seemed an invasion of her privacy. So he was left with one other course of action.

Leaving the hospital at noon on Saturday, he drove into New York, parked and made his way to Bloomingdale's. He knew he was taking a chance; she'd clearly said that she limited the number of bags she supplied to larger department stores. It was possible that he'd find nothing remotely similar to the bag he'd seen. But it was worth a shot, he reasoned, and it was certainly a different way for him to spend his afternoon.

He'd barely approached the handbag counter, when a young saleswoman offered to help him. "Uh, no," he said with a sheepish smile, "I'm just looking." For a full fifteen minutes he surveyed every bag, from those on free-standing racks to those displayed on the counter to those in enclosed cases. Shadowed by the silent saleswoman, he was beginning to feel slightly foolish, when at last he saw something that looked familiar. With effusive praise for his taste, the saleswoman removed the bag from its glass case. It turned out to be Italian-made, with a well-known designer's label stitched inside. When he shook his head, the saleswoman seemed even more disappointed than he, so he dared a description of what he was looking for. She brightened, led him to another case, removed a bag. Again Robert shook his head. Not even close.

"Will you be getting more things in soon?" he asked.

"Not like these. It's the end of the spring season. Within the next month the fall things will start arriving."

"Fall? But it's only June!"

She gave him a sympathetic smile. "After the Fourth of July it's fall in here. So if it's a spring bag you want—"

"No. No, thanks. I guess I'll wait. Thanks for your help." Forcing a smile, he moved off, wondering where next to turn. The nearest Neiman-Marcus was in Westchester, but there were plenty of boutiques in Manhattan. He tried to remember the names his mystery lady had mentioned, but drew a blank. Boutiques, he mused wryly, weren't his specialty.

Swallowing his pride, he retraced his steps to the handbag counter and the young woman who'd helped him moments before. Apologetically he explained that he was trying to locate the maker of the particular type of bag he'd described and that he'd been told that in addition to Bloomingdale's, the bag was sold in various boutiques. Could she possibly suggest a few chic shops where he might look?

She could and did, and he rewarded her with his brightest smile. He never saw her answering blush or the admiring way she stared after him as he headed out the door and down Third Avenue.

One boutique, then another and a third—no luck. Having exhausted the suggestions the young woman had made, he was about to return to his car and head for Westchester, when he saw it. Slung over the shoulder of a willowy mannequin, it had the same braided straps, though in silk rather than leather, the same pieced fabric, though in linen rather than calfskin. Different size. Different shape. Different needlepoint design. But it was . . . distinct.

Eagerly he entered the small boutique. He didn't have to glance at a single price tag to know that both the clothes and accessories were from exclusive fashion houses, and he found himself curiously proud of his mystery lady.

"May I help you?"

"Yes, please. The handbag in your window—the white linen one with the needlework on the front?"

"Ah, yes. It's the last one left. Would you like to see it?"

"Please." He waited patiently while the woman leaned into the front window and slid the bag from the mannequin's shoulder. When she returned with it, he took it in his hands and immediately broke into a smile. There was a *feel* to it—or was the feeling inside him? He wasn't sure, but whatever it was, it was warm and soft and familiar. He turned the bag in his hands, then released the inner snap, never once fearing that he'd find a haughty foreign name inside.

"'Heather,'" he read from the simple but elegant label. Heather. It was perfect. It was her. He looked up. "Do you know Heather?"

"Personally, no. Our buyer does, though. She's been dealing with Heather for several years now."

"Have you ever met her?"

"No. She doesn't come into the shop, or if she does, it's without identifying herself."

Mysterious lady, he thought again. "I understand she lives in Connecticut."

"Uh-huh. She works out of her house and makes each one of the bags by hand. We can't seem to keep them in stock. They sell as soon as they arrive. The only reason this one's still here is that it added so much to the window display that we refused to sell it. But the window dresser's coming to change the display on Monday, so if you'd like this bag, it's yours."

Robert drew his wallet from the inner pocket of his blazer. "I'd very much like it. I'd also like to know a little more about Heather, though."

For the first time the saleswoman grew wary. "I'm not sure I can tell you anything more."

Aware of her hesitance and its possible cause, he smiled. "I'm not trying to steal her away from you. My interest is strictly nonprofessional." When the woman continued to eye him cautiously, he went further. "The fact of the matter is that I met a woman several weeks ago. I never got her name, but in the course of the discussion she mentioned that she was from Chester and that she made handbags. I saw the one she was carrying, and I knew the bag in your window had to be hers. I'd really like to get in touch with her. If you could just tell me her last name—"

"I'm afraid I can't do that. I don't know it myself, and even if I did I doubt I should turn it over to you. If Heather values her privacy, it wouldn't be fair."

"I understand that, but this is important. I assure you I'm no crackpot." He tugged his hospital identification from his wallet. "The name is Robert McCrae. I'm the chief of cardiology at Yale-New Haven."

The woman's eyes widened. "Is there a medical problem?"

"No, no. It's strictly personal." He gave a beseeching smile. "I'd really like to find Heather. Isn't there *something* you can do for me?"

He never knew whether it was his woeful tale, his pleading smile, his hospital ID, or his reputable appearance that convinced the woman. But she excused herself, went into the back room and made a phone call, then returned with the information he wanted.

The next morning, shortly after ten, Heather looked up from where she sat beneath the old apple tree to find Dr. Robert McCrae strolling across her yard.

2

STUNNED, she caught her breath. The doctor from New Haven was the last person she'd expected to see this bright Sunday morning. That he was in her own backyard was all the more astonishing. She was *sure* she hadn't given him her name.

Robert paused several feet away, then closed even that distance and hunkered down beside her. "Are you all right?" Frowning, he brushed her cheek with the back of his hand. "You look pale."

She blinked, feeling a frisson of tension, but also a very visceral excitement. It was, in an odd way, as though a flower were blooming inside her. "I . . . you startled me. I wasn't expecting anyone."

Unable to help himself then, he smiled. It was good to see her, so good. His memory hadn't done her justice. Barefoot, wearing denim shorts and an oversized T-shirt, her dark hair curling gently in the June warmth, she was a heart-stopping sight. Her pallor was already easing, and she looked sweet and fresh and new. "I rang the doorbell, but there was no answer. Since there was a car in the driveway, I figured there had to be someone around, so I came wandering." He eyed the threaded needle in her hand, the small piece of canvas in her lap. "Sunday morning and you're working?"

Heather continued to stare at him. She couldn't believe he was here! "It . . . it was beautiful out and I had stitchery to do . . ."

"You look so comfortable."

She plucked at her T-shirt self-consciously. "If I'd known you were coming, I would have put something nicer on."

"You look great the way you are." Her motion had drawn his attention to the T-shirt, first to the soft, full curve of her breasts, then to the large letters covering them. "'W-H-A-M!'" he read aloud, then sent her a pained look. "I'll say!"

In spite of herself, Heather laughed. "It's a British rock group. Very innocent."

Robert arched a brow as if to say he wasn't quite ready to believe her. "Are you a fan?"

She blushed, then nodded. "Music keeps me company while I work. I'd have a radio on now, except the sounds of the outdoors on a day like this are too good to pass up. Can you hear them . . . the mockingbird over on that tree, the buzzing of a bee . . . or is that a lawn mower down the road?" She grinned, feeling strangely lighthearted. "It doesn't really matter, because in either case the sound fits. And there's a smell in the air of growth and health and warmth. By next month it'll already be older and more mellow."

Robert listened to the sounds and inhaled the smells, but his focus was on Heather. "You're very much a part of this," he observed quietly. "Next to you I feel almost stuffy."

At his words, Heather's gaze slid from his summer blazer to his neatly knotted tie, pressed shirt and creased slacks. "Stuffy" was the wrong word because it implied something negative, when in fact he looked marvelous. "Formal" might have been more correct. And thinking of that word steered her mind onto a more sober track. "Why have you come?" she asked softly, hesitantly.

"I wanted to see you again," he answered simply.

Looking up at him, she felt a flush of pleasure. Only now did she realize that she'd wanted to see him, too. "But . . . how did you find me?"

"A little amateur sleuthing." He settled down on the grass, propped himself on his arms and, stretching his long legs before him, crossed his ankles. "In hindsight, given the outcome, it was actually kind of fun." A mischievous grin had spread across his face. He was obviously pleased with himself, but it was an endearing kind of smugness.

She eyed him suspiciously. "Okay, what did you do?"

"You didn't give me much to work with, but I did manage to locate one of your handbags in a small Third Avenue boutique. The label said Heather. The saleswoman said the rest."

"She shouldn't have—"

"It wasn't her fault. She was reluctant to say a thing, but I pushed."

"Why?"

"Because *you* hadn't contacted *me* and I was getting impatient."

"Impatient . . . for what?" she prodded more guardedly. She wondered if he'd somehow guessed her problem and was thinking medically. She didn't want it to be so. Desperately she wanted it to be the man, not the doctor, who'd come calling.

"I like you, Heather," he said quietly, almost solemnly. "You're different from other people I've known. There's something very...refreshing about you and your work...and this place." He glanced around the yard, and in so doing missed the visible relaxing of her features. "It's lovely here."

She smiled. "Where do you live?" She pictured a functional apartment not far from the hospital, then revised the image to one of an elegant condominium, because there was something distinctly elegant about the man.

He surprised her by saying, "I've got a house in Woodbridge with two acres of land."

She was familiar with the New Haven suburb. It was beautiful. "Then you must be used to grass and trees and wide-open spaces."

He was looking at the branches overhead, his gray gaze seeming almost puzzled. "I should be, but I'm afraid I don't usually take the time to appreciate them. I can't remember the last time I sat on the grass this way."

She glanced at his slacks and tried to picture him in jeans. She wondered if he'd just come from church or the hospital. She hated to think that he'd dressed up just to see her.

"You can't work *all* the time," she ventured cautiously. "You weren't at the hospital today, were you?"

"'Fraid so. But just for a little while, very early." His mouth curved crookedly. "I think the staff looks forward to Sundays because I'm not around much."

"Ahh. So you're an ogre," she teased.

He cleared his throat. "I'm, uh, demanding. Let's leave it at that."

"And what do you usually do on sunny summer Sundays after you've left the hospital?"

He hesitated for a minute, then shrugged guiltily. "Catch up on reading."

"Anything good?" she asked, thinking of the best-selling novel she'd recently finished. If he'd read it, too...

"Medical journals. They're very good."

She whispered a laugh. "To each his own."

"You think I'm crazy."

"No, no. I didn't say that."

"But you're thinking it," he accused good-naturedly. There were the hints of grooves in his cheeks, and she knew he was holding back a smile. Suddenly she yearned to see it full force.

"Okay." She grinned. "I'm thinking it." He did smile then, making her blood tingle through her veins and her cheeks grow pink. To have a man like him smile that way at her was worth any confession. Well... almost. "It's a little like the pot calling the kettle black, though, since you've caught me working on Sunday."

"Actually, it's a relief. It makes me feel less guilty. Now if I had some stuff with me, I'd sit here and read while you worked." He mulled over that prospect for a second. "I kinda like that idea."

She did, too. Very much so. "Do you have your briefcase in your car?" Hadn't he said he'd been at the hospital earlier?

"Sure, but it's packed with files and papers, not journals." And strangely, he wasn't in the mood to look at files and papers. Not with Heather Cole to look at. For that matter, even the journals might have fallen short— a shocking thought, but one he wasn't about to analyze at the moment. "I wasn't sure you'd be here, and I never imagined you'd invite me to work."

"Oh?"

"Most women would take it as an insult."

"I'm not like most women, I guess," she murmured, knowing far more than he the truth of her words. But she didn't want to think about that, not today, not when Robert McCrae's interest was undivided and apparently nonprofessional. "May I, uh, may I get you something cool to drink? It's a pretty warm day." She eyed his necktie, thought of suggesting he loosen it, vetoed that idea as being too forward.

"Not just yet," he mused, unwilling to send her off, out of his sight. He was pleased that she'd accepted his presence as easily as she had. What with her skittishness last time they'd met he hadn't been sure what to expect. But aside from an initial wariness, she was relaxed. He knew he was, which was remarkable. He was away from the hospital, not working, simply sitting outside talking with a woman, and he was relaxed. Remarkable! "Don't let me keep you from working, though," he said almost as an afterthought. "I'd never forgive myself if I disrupted your day."

She put aside the canvas and settled more comfortably against the tree. There was that feeling again . . . that safety . . . and in looks alone, not to mention intelligence and charm, Robert McCrae was as compelling a man as she'd ever known. She had no desire to work at the moment.

"You haven't interrupted me," she said softly. "What doesn't get done today will get done tomorrow. That's part of the beauty of what I do. I make my own deadlines."

"And if you miss them?"

"I miss them. I only work because I enjoy doing it. If the enjoyment goes, I'll stop in a minute."

"Even with the reputation you've established?" When she eyed him questioningly, he explained. "The woman at the boutique said your bags are so popular that they sell as soon as she gets them in. How did you ever get started, anyway? Were you always a crafty person?"

Heather grinned at what she knew to be an innocent, albeit ambiguous, choice of words. "Crafty, never. Good with my hands, always. My parents encouraged me to learn things like sewing and macramé and needlepoint." Her grin faded as she realized that she *was* being crafty, in a way. There was the truth, which she offered, and the whole truth, which she didn't. Quickly she rushed on. "When I found I had an aptitude for that sort of thing, I did more and more."

"How old were you through all this?"

Her hesitation was so brief that it might easily have been tied into the act of recollection. "I started when I was ten. By the time I was a teenager I was addicted."

"How old are you now?" he blurted out, wishing there were a more subtle way to ask but needing desperately to know. Sitting as she was, wearing a WHAM! T-shirt, denim shorts and no makeup at all, she looked to be all of eighteen. His interest in her startled him in many respects, not the least of which was the unpleasant possibility that he might be robbing the cradle or entering some kind of midlife crisis or worse, developing a kinky taste for young flesh. Her answer was everything he wanted to hear.

"Twenty-nine."

His gray eyes widened. "That old?" Then he caught himself and chuckled. "I'm sorry. It's just that you look so much younger sitting here today. The last time I saw you you were dressed up, but even then I wouldn't have guessed you to be more than twenty-six or twenty-seven."

"Thank you . . . I think. How about you? I remember thinking last time that you looked awfully young to be the chief of cardiology anywhere, let alone at Yale-New Haven."

His eyes danced as they held hers close. He was feeling pretty good. "I'm thirty-nine, and thank you, too. It's only been the last three years that I've held the position. I never have figured out whether the hospital deliberately chose someone younger, or whether the older qualified doctors simply preferred private practice."

"Have you ever done that . . . been in private practice?"

"Nope. I like being a staff doctor."

"You must be that much more dedicated."

"How so?"

"Your hours, for one thing. Staff doctors don't take Wednesday afternoons off to play golf, or month-long cruises through the Virgin Islands." She'd carefully kept her tone light, though she had deep feelings on the subject. The doctor she'd seen yearly since her family doctor had moved away was one of those who shuttled patients in and out of his office as though they were on a conveyor belt. He listened to as many hearts as possible in as short a time as possible. And inevitably, when she finally got up the nerve to call for an appointment, it had to be scheduled around one trip or another he was taking. He was an entrepreneur, and she didn't trust him.

Her feelings for Robert McCrae had been different from the start.

"I suppose you're right, there," he was saying, "though it's an overgeneralization. I've known private practitioners who are every bit as dedicated as staff physicians, while there are department heads who delegate authority such that they have time for golf, the Virgin Islands and far more. Personally, I like the action, the excitement of being at the hospital all day. And I like teaching, which is what so much of my work is about. Medical school can go only so far. The real training is done on the floor."

Heather shivered involuntarily. "I'm not sure I'd like the idea of being some novice's guinea pig."

"We work in teams," he explained soothingly, identifying her expression with those so often worn by his patients. Her worry affected him all the more, though, for he was attuned to, captivated by, the slightest change in her features. At the moment her forehead was creased. Her brown eyes were wider, darker, deeper. Her lips were pressed together. "There are no guinea pigs, no experiments. No intern or resident is asked to do something he or she isn't qualified to do and rarely works alone." His gaze lingered on her lips. "Have you ever been to the Virgin Islands?"

Distracted by the intensity of his focus, which sent threads of excitement shimmering all the way to her toes, she struggled to comprehend what seemed to be a non sequitur. "The Virgin Islands?" Her mouth softened into a puzzled half smile. "Where did that come from?"

"We mentioned doctors going to the Virgin Islands. I was just wondering if you've ever been." He loved traveling himself—though his own forays out of state were inevitably professionally oriented—but he recalled she'd commented that first day they'd talked about his having "lived" that much more than she had, and he wondered what she'd meant.

In need of a clear head, she dragged her eyes from his and lowered her gaze, but it fell on his hand lying peacefully in the grass. His fingers were long and lean, squared in a manly way, very beautiful. Not much help in clearing her head. "No. No, I don't travel much."

"Did you when you were a kid?"

"Oh, no," she answered quickly, then steadied her voice. "I mean, I've been to New York and Washington and through a lot of New England, but that's about it. My parents didn't see traveling as a high priority." The full truth was that once her heart condition had been discovered, her parents hadn't considered traveling worth the risk. They'd been frightened of overwhelming her, overburdening her with excitement, not to mention taking her far from the doctor they knew and trusted. More than once she'd suspected they were being overprotective, but she'd said nothing for fear of being proved wrong.

"Then it's not one of your priorities, either?"

She met his gaze. "I didn't say that. I'd love to travel. It's one of my dreams."

"Then why don't you?"

"I guess . . . the right opportunity hasn't presented itself," she answered without lying. She could have taken off by herself on any number of different occasions, but she didn't want to travel alone. The fact was that some of her parents' worry had rubbed off on her. If she'd had someone to travel with, someone to encourage her and assure her that she'd be all right, things might have been different.

"You never travel on business?"

"No."

"That's too bad. It'd probably be fun."

"Actually, it's flattering that the buyers think enough of my work to come here."

"Which brings us back to that. You still haven't told me how you made the jump from hobby to business."

"I'm not sure I have. I still think of what I do as a hobby."

He grinned. "Okay, then, how did you get into selling your hobby?"

At the moment she was far more entranced by the flash of white his grin had allowed than by the chronology of her career. It wasn't that his teeth contrasted boldly with a tan, because he didn't have one to speak of. But he did have good natural color, and his dark hair fell rakishly across his brow, and his body was rangy, stretched out that way on the grass. . . .

"How did I get into selling?" she asked aloud, for her own benefit more than anything else. She took a deep breath and absently plucked a blade of grass from the lawn. "It was kind of a fluky thing. I was a language major in college, and after I graduated I began doing translation work for a professor at Columbia. He'd send me things. I'd translate them, then send them back. It was very convenient, though not as exciting as I'd hoped it would be, and certainly nowhere near as creative. My craft work, on the other hand, was both exciting and creative. I found myself buying little things—a skein of wool or some beads or an interesting pattern—to use as a reward for getting through a translation."

"What kinds of things were you making then?"

"I was weaving belts and rugs, needlepointing pillows and pictures, knotting wall hangings and planters. And I was making most of my own clothes. Then one day I saw something in *Vogue*—a stunning handbag that I was sure I could duplicate and even improve upon."

"And you did."

"I'm not sure I necessarily improved upon it, but I liked what I'd made, so much so that I then made variations to go with different kinds of clothes and color schemes. Wherever I went, I carried one bag or another. People noticed and asked about them. I'd had so much fun making them that when a local shopkeeper asked me to give her several on consignment, I couldn't refuse."

Robert was thoroughly enjoying the story. "And they sold instantly?"

"No." She grimaced playfully. "It was lucky they didn't, actually. Chester proved to be a mediocre market, so several of my bags were still in the shop window when a New York buyer happened to be passing through, and bingo."

"No kidding? It escalated from there?"

"Uh-huh."

"That's a real success story."

"I hope so," she drawled. "It's hard to tell what will happen next year or the year after. Right now women are attuned to what they carry, and they're willing to pay for the right look—through the nose, if you ask me. I'm sometimes appalled when I see the markup on my bags, because I know exactly what the raw materials cost."

Having bought one of her bags, Robert knew the selling price. As far as he was concerned, it was worth every penny. Of course, his motive was far different from that of the average buyer. "But there's your time to consider, and your skill and knowledge of design and style, and the middlemen involved. And you've said yourself that each bag is unique in some small way or another. I'm sure women know exactly what they're getting."

Heather smiled. He was good for her ego. "I hope so."

Basking in her smile, he couldn't look away. In the back of his mind—far, far back where he'd pushed it—was the question of why she'd come to the medical center that first day, why she'd eyed him so nervously. But all he could think about now was how pleasant she was, how free and refreshing, how much he wanted to reach out and touch her.

Heather was thinking similar thoughts. Here with her, in her own backyard, Robert McCrae wasn't a doctor, much less the man she might have approached for personal medical advice. He was thoroughly and unequivocally a man, and one to whom she was strongly drawn. She wanted to reach out and touch him, to comb the fingers of hair from his brow, to trace the faint slashes in his cheeks, to sample the texture of skin that had been shaved several hours before. She wanted to shift places with him, to let him lean against the tree, and then she could relax

against his strong frame. Things that she'd only entertained in fantasy, she suddenly wanted to *do*. Robert
McCrae made her feel soft and attractive and desirable.

"Come, let's take a walk," he said hoarsely. Pushing
himself to his feet, he took her hand and drew her up. He
was so much taller than she, and he held her hand firmly
yet with such gentleness that he made her feel delicate in
a way that was utterly feminine. He didn't release her
hand, and she was glad of it, for his fingers were warm
and strong, his nearness both infinitely comforting and
deliciously arousing. "How long have you had the
house?" he asked as they ambled slowly toward the
woods at the back of the yard.

"I bought it when I graduated from college." Her voice
was breathless. "My parents left me some money and it
seemed the right thing to spend it on."

His thumb lightly rubbed hers. "Did you grow up
around here?"

"In Norwalk. How about you?"

"Long Island. My parents still live there."

Her thigh accidentally brushed his as they walked, and
she felt a ripple of sensual awareness. "Do you have any
sisters or brothers?"

"One of each. And you?"

"Nope. Just me."

He studied her lightly flushed face. "I'll bet you were
doted on as a child."

"Why do you say that?"

"I'd dote on you if you were mine. You evoke that kind
of response."

"The helpless female?" she teased, knowing her parents *had* doted on her, but for a very specific reason.

He stopped walking and brought her to face him. "Just the opposite. You're totally independent. You've got a home and a successful career. You seemed perfectly content with where you were and what you were doing when I came around the corner of your house a little while ago. No, I'd dote on you because attention would be the one thing I could give you that you don't already have."

"There are many things I don't have," she whispered, all but drowning in his shining silver eyes. Her head was tipped up, her body inches away from his. When he released her hand and began to gently stroke her arm, she felt herself leaning closer. Her voice came from a distance. "But you're a busy man. You don't have time to dote on a woman."

His eyes caressed her face. "Maybe I've never been inspired to make the time before."

"Are you now?"

"Oh, yes," he breathed, then lowered his head and brushed his lips against her cheek.

Heather gasped softly. His touch was light but provocative, stirring a myriad of sensations in deep, hidden places. She closed her eyes as he whispered kisses across the bridge of her nose to her other cheek, and she couldn't have moved, much less protested. She was entranced by the strength emanating from him, by his clean, male scent, by the quickening of his breath, which spoke of the effect she had on him.

That in itself was stunning. From the moment he'd arrived, she'd been aware of her own response to him. When he turned those intent gray eyes on her, she tingled; his nearness alone brought her body alive. But that *he* should tremble when he touched her was almost incomprehensible.

"Heather?" he whispered tentatively.

Dazed, she opened her eyes and looked up at him. His fingers slid into her hair, thumbs stroking the faint dampness at her temples. His gaze was heated and direct.

Then his lips sought hers, and all conscious thought fled. There was nothing tentative about his kiss, nothing cautious or halfhearted. His mouth was moist and mobile, his tongue masterful. He possessed her with a sweetness that denied possession, for it evoked a mobility on her part, a seeking, a demand that, if not as forward, was every bit as claim staking.

They were both panting for breath when their lips parted at last. Heather's arms wound about his neck; Robert's encircled her back. He buried his face in her hair; she pressed hers to his throat.

The sun dappled their bodies, playing between branches swaying in the light breeze. It was a warm time, a happy time, and they took advantage of it, standing with their bodies crushed close, their arms sealing the bond. Only when they were in greater control did he ease her back so that he could look down at her face.

"You're something else," he murmured, astonished by the force of what he'd just felt, of what he continued to feel.

"*You* are," she countered in a breathy whisper, her eyes reflecting her own astonishment. She'd been kissed before, but never with such all-pervasive, mind-sweeping force. And she'd *never* responded so openly. Even now, feeling the soft press of her breasts against his chest, she was titillated. Her body seemed a stranger to her, but it was a stranger she wanted to get to know.

Robert saw the look in her eyes and wanted to melt. It had been a long time for him. Maybe that was his problem. Oh, he'd had women since his divorce, but after a number of shallow encounters, he'd stopped forcing himself. With Heather, the only force he had to stop was the one urging him to take her in his arms again, to touch her all over, then to lay her on the grass and make slow, sweet love to her. Even in spite of her volatile response to his kiss, she seemed so fresh, so innocent.

He cleared his throat, but his voice still sounded thick. "I, uh, I think we'd better keep walking. I really didn't come here intending to seduce you."

Heather nodded and released his neck, but she gladly let him tuck her arm through his when they moved slowly on. It occurred to her at that moment that she wouldn't mind at all if he seduced her. Was she wanton to think it, or irresponsible? She'd dated on occasion, but things had never gone beyond minor petting and a goodnight kiss. She'd been frightened then, but she wasn't now.

She tried to analyze what it was about Robert McCrae that made her feel so bold. Though she barely knew him, she liked what she saw. She respected him; he was straightforward and hardworking. And she trusted him. Moreover, there was chemistry between them—she'd never have believed there was truth to that expression had she not felt what she did now.

And, of course, there was that factor of security. Robert was mature, experienced and knowledgeable. He would know what to do, how to take care of her and keep her from harm.

Should she tell him the truth? She didn't want to. Not just yet. She was enjoying the feeling of being healthy and whole. She'd tell him in time, she assured herself. Right now he was making her very, very happy.

"What's that?" he asked, ducking his head and peering through the trees toward a far corner of the yard.

"A tree house." She nudged him in that direction. "Isn't it great?"

They wound through the trees until they were standing at the base of a huge maple. "I don't know. It looks pretty shaky."

"But think of the possibilities," she said with enthusiasm.

That was just what he was doing, without the enthusiasm. He pictured her climbing up the rotted planks, stumbling on one as it crumbled, falling and breaking a leg, or worse. "You haven't been up in it, have you?"

"Oh, no. It was here when I bought the house and I haven't touched it. But I come back here sometimes and sit dreaming about it." She let herself be momentarily drawn into those dreams. "I'd love to have it fixed up one day. It'd be such a perfect hideaway. And if I had children, they'd spend hours playing here."

Studying her animated features, Robert felt the same melting sensation he'd known earlier. In an attempt to escape it, he released her arm and approached the tree. "These rungs are ancient."

"I know." She grinned excitedly. "It makes you wonder when they were nailed up. The house was built around the turn of the century. I can just imagine little kids wearing short pants and high socks and ugly black shoes scampering about."

He looked back at her. She had her hands curved around an overhead limb. Fighting for self-control, he looked away. "Is that what kids wore at the turn of the century?"

"Beats me, but it's fun thinking it, and that's what counts." She studied the tree house. It was primitive, little more than a broad platform built around the trunk and limbs of the tree, and many of the planks were in worse condition than the rungs leading to it. "It's all in the imagination," she mused with a dreamy smile.

Robert, too, was evaluating the condition of the tree house, but distractedly. His immediate dreams were of the woman behind him. He turned his head, noted the slender form of her body, the grace of her arms over her head, the way the pose pertly lifted her breasts. Unable to help himself, he crossed to where she stood, circled her wrists with his hands, then ran them slowly, appreciatively down her arms.

"I think I'm hopeless," he murmured seconds before dipping down to capture her lips. He caressed and sucked, convinced that her honeyed taste was addictive. It flowed through his bloodstream, igniting his nerve ends, feeding his craving in a way that was mind-boggling.

Her response was mind-boggling, as well, for it was pure and open and free. Her lips responded to his slightest prodding, widening when he slid his tongue into her mouth. She was warm and welcoming, all moistness and fire. Yet there was nothing of the wily seductress about her. She was innocence, through and through, even with her hands still grasping the tree limb and her back beginning to arch.

He'd never claimed to be a saint or a martyr. Temptation was a tongued serpent flicking its juices from one end of him to another, until he knew he'd die if he didn't touch her. His hands, which had been cupping her underarms and lifting her nearly off her feet, slid to her front, splaying over her ribs, then moving upward to take the weight of her breasts.

She gasped into his mouth, and he could feel the tremor that shook her, but he only deepened the kiss while his hands explored her turgid flesh. She wasn't wearing a bra, but he'd known that even before he'd sighted WHAM! And he couldn't accuse her of being deliberately provocative, because she hadn't been expecting him. No, she was natural in her untethered state—all the more exciting to him—and her breasts were just crying to be loved.

With a moan, he tore his mouth from hers and pressed it to her forehead. He circled her breasts, stroked them, ran his thumbs over her nipples, and was rewarded when she whimpered softly. When he looked down at her, her eyes were closed. As though feeling his gaze, they slowly opened.

"You're very beautiful," he whispered, dropping his eyes lower to watch her breasts as he shaped them with fingers and palms.

She was breathing shallowly. Her eyes were wide, and he sensed she was stunned by what she was feeling, but there was trust in her gaze, as well. It was that trust that injected a wrinkle of sanity into his burgeoning desire.

With shaky determination, but determination nonetheless, he lowered his hands to her waist.

His voice was hoarse. "I want to touch you, Heather. I want to lift up this T-shirt and see you and feel you. Hell, I want to take off everything and lie down here with you." He paused and closed his eyes for a pained moment. His lower body throbbed, a tight coil needing release. But he couldn't. Not yet. Not so soon. If he didn't fully understand what was happening to him, how could she?

Opening his eyes, he studied her in wonder. "You look so innocent!"

"I am," she whispered, needing to tell him at least that much of the truth. She was clutching his shoulders, but only because her knees felt so weak she feared she might fall. "I've never . . . never done this before." Even to her own ears, the confession sounded stark. Wide-eyed, she awaited his reaction.

His brow furrowed. His thoughts of innocence hadn't gone quite that far. She was twenty-nine and beautiful. How could she possibly have never done this before? "You mean, you're a . . . a . . ."

After a pregnant pause, she nodded. She almost wished she'd said nothing, because at the moment she was feeling strange, but she'd wanted him to know that she wasn't loose, and she'd needed to remind herself of it, too.

"My God, Heather," he exclaimed, hauling her against him and hugging her tightly. "You seemed fresh and new, but I hadn't dreamed—that's wonderful!"

She took strength from him. "You don't mind?"

"Mind? Of course I don't mind!" He held her back and looked into her eyes. Women had reacted to him before, but never with this sense of newness, of preciousness. There was discovery in it. The knowledge that he'd brought her alive as no other man had was no small part of his pleasure. "It makes your response to me all the more special, and what we have is already so explosive!"

"Maybe I shouldn't have said anything—"

He put a finger on her lips. "Don't think that for a minute! I'm glad you told me. The way I feel, the way I react to you, I might have come on too fast or too hard." He pulled her close again, fitting his lower body snugly to hers, and buried his face in her hair, groaning.

With his hips pressed intimately against her, she could feel the hardness of his arousal, and while it was vaguely intimidating, she found intense pleasure in it. She let out a laugh of pure delight. "I think I must be crazy feeling this way, but I'm glad you want me that much. Still it's amazing—I keep thinking I should call you Dr. McCrae." She raised her head. "What should I call you?"

He was beaming at her, eyes crinkled, cheeks slashed, turning her knees to jelly all over again. "Whatever your little heart desires."

"I'm serious.... Robert?"

"Robert. Or Rob. That's what the people closest to me call me, and I'd be proud to put you in that category."

"Then Rob it is," she said with conviction. With her arms around his waist and her body flush to his, she felt strong and wonderful.

She was more than willing to forget she had a problem.

He was more than willing to forget the inkling of a mystery surrounding her.

The day was beautiful, and it was theirs.

"How about that cold drink?" he asked, reluctantly setting her away from him. "I think I could use it right about now."

"You got it," she said brightly, then faltered. "You could also take off your jacket and loosen your tie if you'd like. I wanted to suggest it before, but I wasn't sure how it would sound."

"Sounds pretty suggestive," he drawled, tugging at the knot of the tie.

She tipped up her chin. "But now that you know what an innocent I am, I don't have to feel guilty. You didn't really dress up like that for me, did you?"

"How else should I have dressed?"

"What do you wear when you're sitting at home reading journals?"

"Slacks." With his tie off and the top button of his shirt undone, he was shrugging out of his jacket. Heather was momentarily flustered when what she'd imagined— broad shoulders and lean hips—proved to be even better in reality and exquisitely enticing.

Rob looked down at himself. "When my secretary stares at some part of me the way you're doing, it's usually because I've spilled something or other." He scrutinized his shirt front, then his pants. "I don't see anything."

She jerked her gaze up. "No...uh...it's just that...you look good." Particularly that hair-sprinkled vee of flesh now exposed at his throat. She swallowed hard. "I've never seen you without a jacket."

Grinning, he hooked the item in question over his shoulder and draped his free arm around her. "Most people haven't. See what I do for special ladies?"

They began to walk back toward the house. "Are there others?" Heather asked on impulse.

"Other special ladies? Uh-huh. There's my mother and my sister and, of course, Helen—"

"Who's Helen?"

"My secretary. She'll be relieved I found you. I kept asking her if there'd been a call from Chester. She was beginning to get suspicious."

"I'm sorry. I didn't know—"

"My fault. You hadn't said anything about calling. But still I'd hoped, and since I didn't even know your name . . ."

She changed the subject quickly, not wishing to get into explanations of why she'd been elusive. "But there must be other women. Surely you date."

He squeezed her shoulders. "I work. That's about all I've made time for in the past few years."

She took a minute to savor the feel of his body in step with hers. "Such a waste of manpower," she teased.

"That's what Helen says."

"How old is Helen?"

"Somewhere near sixty."

"Ahh."

He flashed her a grin. "Relieved?"

Her own grin was more sheepish. "Yes. . . . Am I awful?"

"You're wonderful."

"But I sound possessive. I've never been possessive in my life."

"I'm not complaining. Given what happened a little while ago, you've got every right to want to know where you stand. Haven't I asked you similar questions?"

"I suppose.... How about friends? Do you have lots?"

"That depends on your definition of a friend."

With a half smile she grew philosophical. "There are two kinds, I think. The first, a friend with a small 'f,' is one you see from time to time, maybe go to a restaurant or a show with, talk with about general things. The relationship is inspired in a large part by either physical proximity or some particular interest in common."

"And the second kind?"

"A friend with a capital 'F' is one you trust implicitly, one you go out of your way for and one who'll go out of his or her way for you, one you might choose as a relative if relatives could be chosen. A big 'F' friend is someone you share deeper things with, emotional things like feelings and dreams."

"Then I've got lots of the first and very, very few of the second."

She thought about it for a minute. "Isn't that true for most men?"

"As opposed to women? I think so."

"It's a cultural thing."

"But physical, as well, if you want to be really philosophical about it. A woman is built to share. Look at what she does for an unborn child during the period of gestation."

"That kind of physical sharing is different, though. It's unconscious."

"But isn't it possible that it accounts for the female animal's predilection to openness? Men aren't naturally like that. They should be. But they aren't." They'd reached the house and were climbing the few steps to the screened-in back door. He stopped at the top and turned to her, speaking quietly, intently. "I've always been a loner, Heather. It's not easy for me to tell people things about myself. I'm not used to that kind of sharing, which was one of the reasons I had to see you again. I blurted things out to you last time—things about my marriage and the kids—well, not many people at the hospital know they even exist. I'm still not sure why I told you. Maybe there's a need in me that I haven't been willing to acknowledge."

"Why not?"

He shrugged. "My work has always come first. Even before medicine, I was intensely involved in whatever it was I was doing at the time. I was a bookworm as a kid, and when I got to college I was a nonstop studier."

"There's nothing wrong with that."

"No. I was happy. Once I got to med school, there was that much more to do, to learn. I married because it seemed the thing to do, part of the image, if you know what I mean." When she nodded her understanding and acceptance, he went on. "But there was another part of the image, that of being strong and self-contained. As a doctor, I've been constantly busy, and successful enough to believe that I'm in control of every aspect of my life. Maybe that's why I've ignored any need for sharing in my personal life."

"But you sense the need is there?"

"I'm talking to you, aren't I? I'm not sure I understand it, but you seem to inspire that kind of opening up." He ran a hand through his hair. "Maybe it's because you're alone. We have that in common. I feel I can trust you."

"I'm glad," she said, meaning it.

Smiling gently, he gave her shoulder a squeeze. "Enough seriousness. Are you going to show me the inside of your house, or am I going to have to break and enter?"

She pulled open the screen. "Since there's nothing to break, you can enter with impunity. I'll get you that drink. Then I'll show you around."

Moments later, having downed tall glasses of lemonade, they wandered through the house. "I'm amazed!" Robert exclaimed, trying to take everything in at once. "It's so modern!"

"Surprised you, huh?"

"I'll say! Some turn of the century house! Was it this way when you bought it?"

"Not quite. I wish I had 'before' pictures to show you. It was pretty old and run-down, but I couldn't resist the basic design of the place. You don't get arched windows and tiny alcoves and twisting staircases anymore."

"Or high ceilings, for that matter."

They were in the living room, which was open and bright. "This room was originally two. I had the dividing wall taken down." She chortled. "In fact I had lots of walls taken down. I didn't want ten small rooms, when five large ones would be that much more pleasant."

"And you haven't cluttered the place with furniture. I can breathe here."

She gave him a facetious look. "Some people would say I haven't *bought* furniture yet. The way I see it, a sofa and two chairs, a few tables and a stereo are all I need."

Robert agreed, though he could see that the sofa, chairs, end tables and stereo were of the finest quality and taste, as was the artwork that hung on select walls and carried through the pale blues, apricots and whites of the room.

He grabbed Heather's hand. "Show me the rest. I'm intrigued."

Dutifully but excitedly she showed him the dining room, then the three rooms upstairs. One was her bedroom, with a modern brass bed, a sitting area and a dresser and dressing table. The second was a library, boasting floor to ceiling bookshelves, a cushiony upholstered sofa and a large rya rug. The third was her workroom.

"My pièce de résistance," she announced with delight. "A little messy, but I make no apologies for that."

"You shouldn't," he commented, taking in the shelves piled with fabrics and yarns in a wild array of colors, the long worktable similarly strewn, the sewing machine, elaborate cassette player and easy chair. "I assume you had the skylights put in yourself. The slanted roof is made for them."

"They were the first priority when I started renovating—well, after electricity and plumbing. I like things to be bright and cheerful. If this room had been at the front of the house I might have had qualms. I didn't want to do anything to detract from the period look of the exterior."

"But it's at the back, so you don't have to worry."

"And I get the morning sunshine, which I love."

"You're a morning person, too?"

"Uh-huh."

"Not a 6:00 A.M. worker."

"Sometimes.... What do you do at that hour? Isn't it a little early for rounds? I'd think your patients would be sleeping."

"They are. More often than not I have breakfast with my interns and residents. It's a perfect time to discuss cases. Either that, or I spend the time in my office going over things or dictating notes or letters into a machine so Helen can type them up when she gets in."

"Very efficient."

"Mmm." But he didn't want to think about the hospital. "Do you always go around barefoot? You look like a sprite."

She tempered a grin. "It's comfortable."

"You could slip on these wood floors."

"I don't move very fast."

He arched a brow. "Excuse me?"

"I said that I don't move . . . very fast." She sent him a sideways glance. He was smiling mischievously. "Why are you looking at me that way?"

"Because you took those stairs as though there were wings on your feet. Listen to you. You're breathless even now."

"That's from excitement," she informed him pertly. She refused to be reminded of the other possible cause, and she *was* excited. "It's not every day that I get to show such a renowned guest around my home."

"Renowned, baloney." Without warning, he swooped down and took her mouth in a searing kiss. For a blissful eternity their lips clung, though no other part of their bodies touched.

When they separated, Heather was more breathless than ever. Her only consolation was that Rob was in a like state. He wore a pained expression as he wound his fingers through her hair. "This is going to be very difficult, I think."

"What is?" she whispered. It all seemed so natural and easy.

"Being close to you and keeping my libido in check." He leaned forward to nuzzle her cheek. His praise came out in a moan. "You smell so good. What is that?"

"Moisturizing lotion," she murmured. All she could smell was the clean male scent emanating from Rob, and it was doing unnerving things to her equilibrium.

His lips were nipping at her earlobe, then her neck. "It's here, too."

She gasped when his tongue touched the hollow of her throat. "It's all over."

Images of her breasts, her belly, the small of her back, her thighs smoldered through his brain. With a groan, he straightened and took several deep, deep breaths.

Heather hadn't realized she'd closed her eyes until they blinked open. She watched him, waiting, wanting, wishing she had the nerve to take the initiative and kiss him. But she wasn't quite that bold. Not yet.

Then she tipped her head and grew alert. "What's that?"

"My lungs. They're laboring."

"No, no." She moved toward the door. "There's a noise. Not the phone. A beeper—do you have a beeper?"

"In my jacket downstairs." He was at the door, passing her, starting down the stairs. "You've got some ears.

I never would have heard it. You know, I can't remember when that's ever happened to me!"

Heather felt guilty, but not because she'd distracted him. No, she felt guilty because she wished he hadn't heard the beeper at all! She knew it was selfish of her, but she'd never been particularly selfish and one perverse part of her said she'd earned the right to be, for once.

When she reached the kitchen, where Rob had left his jacket, she found him staring at the now silent beeper. "What do you have to do?" she asked softly.

He sighed and looked up apologetically. "I'll have to call in."

"What does it mean when your beeper goes off? That a patient's in trouble?"

"Possibly. May I use your phone?"

She gestured toward the instrument, hanging on the wall.

Rob lifted the receiver, dialed in for his message, then phoned the appropriate floor at the hospital to learn more about the patient who'd gone into cardiac arrest. All the while he watched Heather. Her eyes were worried; she bit her lip from time to time, picked at a fingernail.

When at last he hung up the phone, she swallowed. "You have to leave."

He nodded.

"Is it serious?"

"The patient's okay now, but it's been touch and go for a long time, and this is very definitely a setback. He had a triple bypass three years ago, and it looks like he may need another. Since he's been a patient of mine all this time, I want to get in and reassure him. The psychological ramifications of something like this thing are rough. I'd also like to talk with the surgeon."

"You mean . . . you don't do the surgery yourself?"

"I leave that to the specialists."

Heather was taken aback. "But I thought you were a specialist."

"Not in surgery."

She said nothing more. This latest twist would take some getting used to.

Rob slipped his blazer on, then turned to her. "I'm sorry to be running out this way, Heather. I would have liked to spend more time with you. Can I give you a call?"

She nodded.

He took a step forward, then stopped. He wanted to kiss her a final time, but he suddenly felt guilty. His work was his life. It wouldn't be fair to involve her in something that could be part-time at best, in reality little more than a few hours stolen here and there. He'd disappointed Gail that way. Could he do the same to Heather?

Knowing only that he didn't want to hurt her, he gave her a sad smile, then turned and left.

3

AT SEVEN O'CLOCK that night the phone rang. Heather snatched it up without pretense. "Hello?"

"Heather? It's Rob." His voice was deep, softening even as he spoke. "How are you?"

With a smile of relief, she reached over to lower the stereo, then sat back in her chair. "I'm fine. And you?"

"Fair to middlin'." Better now that he'd heard her voice. By the time he'd gotten home from the hospital, he was wondering if he'd imagined the morning.

"How did it go?" she asked cautiously.

"Okay. We've got him scheduled for surgery in the morning."

"What are his chances?"

"Not bad, actually. He was in pretty good spirits when I left him, and that's part of the battle."

"Will you be there during the surgery?"

"I'll be at the hospital."

"But not in the operating room?"

"No. I'll be kept up to date, and I'll see him as soon as he comes out of anesthesia."

"What will you be doing while they're operating?"

"What I usually do. I start rounds at seven or so. Then I'll see outpatients for a while, and I've got a couple of administrative meetings scheduled around noon."

"And the afternoon?"

"More meetings. More patients. Plus plenty of desk work—correspondence, research reports, that type of thing—then evening rounds." He paused. "You're full of questions."

She heard his smile and, picturing it, felt better. "I was curious. I've been sitting here trying to imagine what you do."

"And I've been sitting here imagining you in that workroom of yours. Are you there now?"

"Uh-huh."

"Working?"

"I finished the piece I started this morning, so I began another."

"I heard music before. What were you listening to?"

"Duran Duran."

"Come again?"

Her lips curved up. "Duran Duran."

"Oh. Okay."

"They're really good. 'Wild Boys.'"

"Are they?"

She laughed. "That was the song that was on."

"'Wild Boys'?" he echoed dubiously. "No wonder I've never heard it. I wouldn't be able to identify. I've never been wild in my life."

"That's okay. Most pop music is fantasy, anyway. I usually prefer more of a ballad sound, but this one's got a good beat. It talks of wild boys who shun glory... reckless boys...hungered boys. It's slightly naughty, but naughty is fun to think about sometimes." As was true of most of the music she listened to, she derived vicarious pleasure from it. The lyrics held romance and adventure. Sometimes she'd stand and sway to the beat, more often she'd simply listen . . . and dream.

"I can't believe you've ever been naughty."

"You're right."

"But you like the song."

"Uh-huh."

He wondered if she'd ever *wanted* to be naughty, but refrained from asking. "Fair enough," he conceded, settling more comfortably in his seat. "Did you go back outside after I left?"

"For a while. I barbecued chicken for lunch. I'm sorry you weren't able to stay and have some. It was good."

"Do you like to cook?"

"Love to. I'm kind of a low-salt, low-fat, low-cholesterol gourmet cook." Realizing afterward what she'd said, she held her breath.

"A health nut?"

Relieved that he'd taken her quip lightly, she let out the breath. "I believe in sensible eating. What is it they say— a woman can't be too thin or too rich?"

"You're thin enough." He pictured her as he'd seen her that day. She was slender, with subtle curves in all the right places. His thoughts homed in on her breasts. Unconsciously he pressed his thighs together. "I like the way you feel."

A blush stole through her body. "Thank you," she murmured softly. When he'd been there, kissing her, touching her, she hadn't felt shy, but once he'd left, the newness of what had happened had hit her. Even now she couldn't believe she was talking on the phone so softly, almost intimately with Robert McCrae. For there *was* something intimate about their conversation, not in words as much as tone. She remembered the many times she'd envied young lovers she'd passed in town or the park, remembered the way their heads were bent together, the way they'd seemed to be murmuring sweet nothings. This phone conversation was as close as she'd ever felt to that.

"Do you have a full twenty bags to put out this week?" Rob asked.

"Uh-huh. The stores are clamoring for the fall things."

He grunted. "That's what the lady at Bloomingdale's told me, but it still seems slightly insane. What happens, come mid-July, if you want to buy something to wear for that weekend?"

"You dig into your closet and make do with second best. It is a little crazy. I had to learn the hard way not to wait till the last minute to buy summer things."

"You don't still make your own clothes?"

"I don't have time. And even if I did, I can't make something like, say, a bathing suit. Heaven help the woman who decides she needs a new one in the middle of the summer. There's nothing in the stores."

"So you've already bought a bathing suit. What's it like?"

"Uh . . . it's very simple." Skimpy was what she might have called it, but she was self-conscious.

Not so Rob. He was intrigued. "One piece? Two piece?"

"Two."

He moaned softly, but the torture was bliss. "Teeny?"

"It's . . . simple."

"What color?"

"Bright yellow with blue polka dots."

"You're kidding."

"No, I'm not."

"How can you do this to me, Heather?"

"You asked."

"Mmm. I did, didn't I. Maybe you'll let me see it sometime?"

"Sure," she teased, feeling bolder by the minute. There was something surprisingly pleasant about wielding feminine power. She'd never had the experience before, and though she doubted she'd want a steady diet of it, it was momentarily heady. "It's hanging right in my closet on an itty-bitty hanger."

"I don't want to see it on a hanger," he growled. "I want to see it on you."

"And what will *you* be wearing? I'll feel pretty silly if you've got on a tie and jacket." She was probing, wondering what he was wearing right then, but reluctant to ask. She feared he'd say slacks, and though she knew he'd still look super, she wanted to think that he owned jeans or shorts, something strictly casual.

"I suppose I could pick up something."

"Come on. You have a bathing suit, don't you?"

There was a moment's silence on his end of the line, then a pensive, "I think I've got one at the bottom of a drawer somewhere. I haven't been to a beach since I left California, and then it was only once or twice with the kids."

"Shame on you, Rob. The beach is such fun."

"Do you go often?"

"Whenever I can. There's nothing like lying in the sun, listening to the sounds of laughter and the roll of the waves."

"Do you swim?" He imagined her stroking gracefully through the surf, diving smoothly, resurfacing with her face to the sun and her hair streaming back.

"No," she answered more softly. "I don't swim."

"Didn't you ever learn?"

"When I was little. But I haven't done much more than wade in years."

"Shame on you, Heather. Swimming is the best exercise in the world. For a woman who's a nut for good nutrition, there's something slightly contradictory here."

Not at all, she was thinking. She was also thinking that it would be fun to swim. Her parents had frowned on her exerting herself in any way, and she'd let herself believe they were right. So swimming and bicycling and jumping rope had ended. Not that she cared to jump rope now, but to swim . . . or to bicycle . . .

"I'd swim with you if you were game," she ventured cautiously. She couldn't forget how busy he was, and she didn't want to demand time he didn't have to spare.

"Maybe we'll do that one day," he surprised himself by saying. He was already trying to figure out when he might squeeze such a day into his schedule, but . . . hadn't he been prepared to take today off and spend it with her? "I'll probably be pretty rusty," he warned.

"No more so than me," she returned happily, feeling a little—but only a little—like a child who'd been promised cotton candy. The grown woman in her was excited at the thought of seeing Rob in swim trunks, of his seeing her in a bikini, of their spending even a short time together at the beach.

Rob was astonishingly attuned to her happiness. It occurred to him that he wanted to make her happy, to see her smile. Yes, she seemed content with her life, but little things she'd said and done made him suspect that her contentment only went so far. She was alone. Yet she didn't seem to want to be. Actually, he didn't want her to be, either.

"If I can get someone to cover for me some Sunday soon, we'll go. How does that sound?"

"Can you do that?" she asked hopefully.

"Damn it, if I haven't earned the right to a day off now and again, I'm doing something wrong," was his answer. It was very much his inner thought spoken aloud, an argument made for his own benefit.

"I'd love that, Rob."

"Good," he said huskily. "I'll work on it. And speaking of work, I'd better run. There's a lot I've got to get through before I reach the hospital in the morning. If I'm not prepared for the day, my image will be torn to shreds."

"I can't imagine that ever happening," she chided.

It was already happening, at least in his own mind. He was somewhat confounded by what he'd discovered with Heather. Had he actually offered to get someone to cover for him? Sure, it happened all the time when he had to leave town, but that was official business. This? This would be . . . pleasure. And pleasure, separate and apart from his profession, was something new to him.

"How about if I call you in a few days?" he asked quietly.

"I'd like that."

"Well . . . take care, Heather."

"You, too, Rob. And good luck tomorrow."

"Thanks." He wanted to say more, didn't want to let her go just yet, but he had much to think about, and, yes, work to do. So, with a soft-spoken, "Bye-bye," he hung up the phone.

HE MADE IT until Wednesday without calling, and that only with great willpower. Though he'd poured himself into his work, he'd thought about Heather, too, such that by the time he heard her voice it simply wasn't enough.

"I'm going to be finishing up here in an hour or so," he told her. "That'll make it about seven o'clock. Can I drive up and take you out to dinner?"

Heather felt that the waiting had all been worthwhile. She'd repeatedly reminded herself of how busy Rob was, how demanding and important his work was, how rewarding it was to him. A simple phone call would have delighted her. A dinner invitation was heaven!

"You can drive up, but wouldn't you rather have dinner here? You're probably exhausted, and the drive here is long enough without having to continue on to a restaurant."

"But that would mean work for you."

"I love to cook, remember? I was just about to fix something for myself. It'd be simple to make it for two."

The prospect of a home-cooked meal, a Heather-cooked meal, was a hard one to turn down. "Are you sure?"

"Positive. I'll see you later, then?"

"Great. And listen, if you decide you don't want to cook, after all, just think up a nice place to go. I won't mind."

"I will." She wanted him all to herself. "See ya later."

She hung up the phone with stars in her eyes, so excited that her heart was pounding. Taking several deep breaths, she forced herself to calm down. It wouldn't do, she reflected, to be ill by the time he arrived! As it was, she felt like a heel for not telling him the truth about herself. But she'd thought about it and thought about it and decided that no harm would come if she waited just a little longer. Just a little longer. That was all. She was too happy right now to throw a monkey wrench in the works.

Carefully pacing herself, she took out the makings for Florentine chicken, a salad and rice. When the initial preparations were done, she set the dining room table with the china, silver and crystal that had been her mother's.

"You'd like him, Mom," she said aloud. "He's such a good person, and I'm safe with him. Safe and secure!"

With that declaration, she raced—caught herself and walked upstairs to shower. She brushed her hair until it gleamed, lightly applied makeup, then put on a fresh yellow sundress and sandals. By the time she returned to the kitchen, she was grateful to have cooking to occupy her.

She was nervous. It had been months since she'd had a date, and this was the first time she'd ever invited a man for dinner. The fact that it wasn't just any man coming, but Rob, was both comforting and unsettling. She wanted everything to be right—the food, the house, her. She wanted to impress him. She wanted to appear as worldly as he seemed. She wasn't sure if she could pull if off . . . but she was determined to try.

The worst moment was that first one when she opened the door. It didn't matter how often she'd pictured Rob in her mind, seeing him, so straight and tall and handsome, feeling his compelling presence at her threshold, shook her. She felt shy and unsure, but only until he spoke.

"Hi," he said softly, his gray eyes glowing.

"Hi," she breathed, returning both his greeting and his smile.

"You look great."

"So do you."

He cocked his head. "But I'm wearing my standard outfit. Yours is special."

She blushed. "It's just a dress."

"It looks wonderful on you."

"I didn't want to look eighteen again."

"You don't. You look twenty-two."

She rolled her eyes, stood back and gave a playful growl. "Come on in."

"I stopped for some wine." He held up a telling narrow bag. "Okay if I put it in the refrigerator?"

"I'll do that," she offered, but before she could relieve him of the wine he was on his way into the kitchen.

"No need. Anyway, my nose is leading me onward." He dragged in an exaggerated breath. "Something smells great."

Heather leaned back against the counter and watched as he bent to lay the wine on its side on a shelf. She rather liked his making himself at home here. "It's chicken. It'll be ready soon."

Closing the refrigerator, he rubbed his hands together. "I can't tell you when I last ate an honest to goodness home-cooked meal."

"Then I'm doubly glad I insisted we eat here. Do you really go to restaurants all the time?"

"Not necessarily."

"So you do cook."

"Nothing I'd consider an actual meal."

She grinned. "What do you make?"

He was leaning against the counter at right angles to her. "I can fry an egg and toast bread and boil water for instant coffee. I'm great at opening cans—tuna, beef stew, soup. Between frozen dinners and other precooked concoctions, I survive."

"Do you have someone in to clean your house?"

"Once a week. It doesn't get very dirty with just me in it. I'm pretty much house-trained."

"So you do put the dishes in the dishwasher when they're dirty?"

"Uh-huh. I also run laundry through when I have to."

She was trying not to grin again. "I'm impressed."

"You are not. I know that smug-woman look. You're thinking that I'm just another helpless man around the house."

"No, I'm not. Really. Besides, even if I were, what difference would it make? Given the status you've attained in medicine, it wouldn't matter if you never lifted a finger at home."

"But it would," he said, growing more serious. "It matters very much nowadays. Society expects much more of men than it used to. It's no longer acceptable simply to go to work and come home with a paycheck.

If a man enters into a relationship, he's got to be willing to share the responsibility for it."

"You're not talking about cooking and housecleaning."

"No." He paused, frowned, pressed his forefinger to a point of tension between his eyes before finally looking back at Heather. "I've been thinking about it since Sunday."

"About what?" she whispered.

"About what I want with you."

"And . . . ?"

"I want something, Heather, but I don't know how much and I don't know if it'll work. I feel torn between the man I've always been and the man I might like to be."

"The man who works all the time and the one who has time for other interests?"

"I suppose that says it, but even then . . . What woman wants to be an 'other interest'?"

Heather shrugged. "Maybe one who has nothing else," she wanted to say, but she knew that would sound both self-pitying and slightly desperate, and she didn't like to think of herself as either. "Maybe one who's like you. A woman who has a satisfying career of her own, but feels it might be nice to have something more once in a while."

"You're not that way. Once in a while isn't enough. You want a husband. You want children."

She couldn't lie. On the other hand, she wanted him to know that her demands were few. "Yes. But even then I want to have my work. You're right, Rob. Society does expect more from men nowadays. But it also expects more from women, or maybe it just allows more." She paused. What she was about to say might sound presumptuous, but she was willing to take that chance. She didn't know Rob well—this was only the third time she'd seen him. Yet, given the way she felt when she was with him, she wanted there to be a fourth, a fifth time. "I'd never ask more than you could give. I'm not looking for a constant companion." Or a nursemaid, God forbid. Her parents had been enough. "I'm not sure I could stand that. Don't forget. I've lived alone for seven years now. I'm set in my ways, too."

"You'd be flexible."

"I'd try."

His expression grew pained. "But what if I could only offer you one night a week? What if we had plans and I had to cancel at the last minute when an emergency came up? What if something happened at the hospital and I was distracted, thinking about it even when we were together?"

She smiled gently. "I think I'd be proud enough of who you are and what you do to try to understand."

He let out a long breath. "You're too good, Heather. You deserve more."

"'More' is a relative concept." When one started from scratch, "more" could be very little. "I'm not asking for the world."

"What are you asking for?"

Good health. Companionship. Love. She looked down. "Friendship, for starters. A phone call now and then would be nice."

"And after that?"

"Time together. It doesn't have to be a whole lot." She raised her eyes. "I think that more than anything I'd like to know I mean something to someone, that he thinks of me from time to time in the course of his work. And I'd like to have someone to think about, too. It's the quality of affection, not the quantity that matters."

Rob stared at her almost in disbelief. She was so easy, so comfortable, so forgiving. She had all the right answers. But if he entered into an ongoing relationship with her, he'd feel a responsibility toward her. Hell, he felt it already. The question was whether he was up to it.

The problem was that he did want her. Not only physically, but—to some extent or another—emotionally, as well.

"I can't promise much, Heather. I am what I am."

"I know that."

"I've never been good at lasting relationships."

"Nothing lasts forever," she said more sadly. Though her physical ailment had never been particularly life threatening, it had certainly made her consider her own mortality.

"True." Pushing himself from the counter, not once taking his eyes from hers, he came to where she stood and put his hands on either side of her neck. "Then you're willing to give it a go?" he asked softly.

There was no need for hesitation. Wordlessly she nodded.

His thumbs stroked the underside of her jaw, while his gaze roved her features. Then he tipped her face up and lowered his own, and he kissed her once, then again, then a third time, with growing ardor.

Heather shared the ardor. She'd gotten used to the fact that she was physically attracted to Rob, yet the force of that attraction never failed to amaze her. At his slightest kiss she was reduced to putty, molding and shaping to him in a way that prompted an even greater response from him.

"I could stand here all night kissing you," he murmured thickly.

"I'm not complaining," she breathed, entranced.

"You should be. Your chicken will burn."

"No, it won't. It's got a little while to go yet. I wasn't sure exactly when you'd get here."

Flexibility. Intuitively he'd known she'd offer it. Now he wondered how far it would go. He slid his arms around her back and pressed closer. "Then I can kiss you again?"

"If you'd like."

"I'd like," he growled. "I'd like very much."

So he did. He kissed her thoroughly, deeply, exploring the recesses of her mouth with his tongue while his hands roamed ever more restlessly over her back, her shoulders, her upper arms. He leaned into her, needing to feel more. Then, needing to touch more, he levered his upper body away.

Heather was helpless to deny him anything. It felt too good, too right, his kissing her, leaning into her, touching her. Her body tingled. Her mind whirled. She gave herself up to the pleasure she'd never known but always dreamed about.

"So soft," he murmured against her lips when his hands rose from her waist to cup her breasts. "So soft and full." She was swelling into his touch, her breath quickening along with his. "But you're wearing a bra," he whispered.

"I know." The regret in her voice was faint but obvious.

His fingers continued their sensuous kneading, and his lower body was growing more taut by the minute. He settled himself more snugly against her, his voice nearly as weak as hers had been. "You weren't last time."

"I wasn't expecting you last time," she gasped, then moaned when his fingers found her nipples and began to stroke them gently. "Rob!" His name was a ghosted exclamation on her lips.

"Feel good?"

She was clutching his shoulders, her fingertips digging into his blazer. "Oh, yes!"

"I'd like it, too," he whispered.

Her head came up, eyes flying open. She watched him take one of her hands, press it flat, then slide it from his shoulder, over his collarbone to his chest.

"Touch me," he coaxed in that same hoarse whisper. "I want to feel you touching me, too." He guided her hand in a slow circle, all the while watching surprise and pleasure light her face. Soon he didn't need to guide, for she'd begun exploring on her own, and it was everything he could have asked and more. He closed his eyes and dropped his head forward, concentrating on the feel of her palm, then its mate, against him.

For Heather it was a time of blissful discovery. He was strong. Lean muscles rippled beneath her touch. She spread her fingers and, through his shirt, felt the spring of his chest hair, which in turn sparked tiny curls of fire deep inside her. She'd been so wrapped up in what he'd been doing to her that she hadn't thought to touch him, but she was so glad he'd led her, so glad. Even had her own body not tingled in response, the look of sheer pleasure on his face would have been reward enough.

Growing bolder, she focused on the hard dots beneath her fingertips. She stroked them as he'd done hers, and his shudder echoed through her.

He moaned, took a ragged breath, knew that if he didn't somehow stop her he'd soon be encouraging her to take far greater liberties with his body. She was willing. He knew she was. He also knew that she was a virgin, and he felt the burden of that responsibility.

Moaning again, he put an end to her caresses by wrapping his arms around her back and drawing her hard against him. He doubted any woman had ever been so soft, so warm, so giving. He doubted he'd ever wanted any woman as badly as he wanted Heather.

"Enough," he groaned. "We have to stop."

"Why? If it felt good—"

"It felt too good. I didn't come here tonight to seduce you."

"That's what you said last time."

"And I meant it. But I can't seem to control myself when I'm with you. I have to keep reminding myself that you're a virgin."

Heather stiffened. "What does that have to do with it?"

"It's a very important fact."

There was defiance in her gaze when she drew her head back to look up at him, but it was a defiance born of embarrassment and, even more, of frustration. Her body was throbbing, most notably around the pit of her stomach. She wanted...more! "I shouldn't have told you. If I hadn't said anything, you wouldn't be holding back."

Thinking that she looked all the more seductive in anger, he gave her a crooked grin. "You're probably right."

"It doesn't matter, Rob. I'm an adult. It's not as though I've saved myself on principle."

"Then why are you still a virgin?"

His directness took her aback, and she wished she could give him the whole truth. She couldn't. Half of it would have to do. "Because...because I've never wanted it before."

"And you're sure you want it now."

"I . . . yes."

"How can you be? You barely know me!"

Pushing herself from his light grasp, she stalked across the room, then whirled to face him. "You wanted me," she stated accusingly. "I could feel it."

"Men can't hide that kind of thing."

"Just because women can doesn't mean they feel it any less. You wanted me, didn't you?"

"I wanted you the first time I laid eyes on you."

"How could you?" She threw his words back in his face. "You barely knew me!"

He stared at her in disbelief for a minute, then lowered his head and rubbed the back of his neck. "You're too quick, Heather. You know just what to say." Slowly he raised his eyes. "But it won't change my mind. At least, not right now. When the time's right, it'll be right. And we'll both know it."

As Heather stood facing him, her defiance faded. He was only doing what he believed to be right. How could she be annoyed, when his expression bore such tangible regret? How could she feel humiliated, when he'd admitted he wanted her, when he'd admitted he wanted a relationship with her?

A sheepish smile crept onto her lips. "Is there hope for the future?"

"Very definitely, I'd say." He took a step toward her.

"And you don't think I'm terrible for wondering?"

He took a second step. "I think that you're a very normal, healthy woman." And a third. "Who's got great taste in men."

"I think that if you come much closer your entire argument will be for naught."

"Y'do, do you?" he asked, grinning. But he didn't come any closer.

She cocked her head. "I do. On the other hand, if you'd like to make yourself useful, you can get the corkscrew from that drawer over there—" she gestured "—and uncork the wine while I see if the chicken's done."

"Wine? Wine. Good thought. I could use some."

"Good thoughts?"

"Wine, Heather. Wine."

Their simultaneous chuckles set the mood for the dinner that followed. Conversation flowed smoothly between them, dealing primarily with what each had done during the few days since they'd last been together.

Heather got more of a glimpse of Robert's professional life, learning that he taught at the medical school two afternoons a week, that he was the director of a research team, that he'd just completed a new article on his own to be published in the *New England Journal of Medicine*, that his closest friends at the hospital were Howard Cerillo, his second in command in cardiology, and Jason Parrish, the chief of psychiatry.

Rob learned that Heather took regular weekday walks into the center of Chester and that if she missed more than two or three days she immediately received a concerned call from Ruth Babcock, a grandmotherly type who lived along the way and had a never-ending supply of apple cider waiting. He also learned that she lunched from time to time with Beth Windsor, a local bookseller whose shop she frequented, and that she'd become close friends with Elaine Miller, the buyer who'd first seen her handbags in the Chester shop window.

The evening sped by, and before Heather was willing to let it end, Rob was on his feet, taking her hand, heading for the door.

"We've both got to work tomorrow," he said by way of apology, and his gaze elaborated. "It's getting late, and you look tired."

"I'm fine," she insisted. Though it was nearly eleven and she was usually asleep by ten, she would have gladly entertained Rob for as long as he'd been willing to stay. But she knew enough not to prod. After the talk they'd had before dinner, the last thing she wanted to do was to complain that he had to leave.

"Let me see what I can do about this weekend," he said, slipping his arms around her. He was proud of the control he'd exercised from dinner on, resisting the urge to hold her, to kiss her and more. He knew, though, that he couldn't leave without feeling her body against his once more, so he drew her close and hugged her tightly. His pleasure was intensified when she fitted her arms comfortably around his back. "I'll give you a call on Friday. Okay?"

Heather smiled against his chest. That was all she wanted at the moment—to know that he'd be calling and when. It gave her something to look forward to. "Sounds great."

He kissed her once, very lightly, then left. She watched him back his BMW out of the driveway, waiting until its taillights vanished into the night before closing the door. Glowing with happiness, she turned out the lights, went upstairs and fell promptly to sleep.

"Sure, I'll cover for you Sunday," Howard Cerillo said without hesitation. "What's up?"

Rob shrugged. "Up? Nothing. I just wanted to have a free day."

"Something's up."

"Nothing's up."

Howard looked skeptical. "Are you sure?"

"Of course I'm sure."

Howard scratched the back of his head and tried to suppress a smile. "How long have we known each other?"

"Six years."

"Right. We've been working together that long, and this is the first time you've asked me to cover for you."

"You've covered for me lots of times."

"Sure. When you've been out of town. Never simply for the sake of a 'free day.' Not that I mind, Rob. You've certainly done it enough for me." His eyes narrowed into slits of amusement. It wasn't often that he had a chance to tease Robert McCrae. As a friend, he sensed something was very definitely up. As a man, he suspected what it was. "Is she gorgeous?"

"Who?"

Seeing Rob go red, Howard knew he was on the right track. "The woman you're going to see?"

"Who said I was seeing anyone?"

"Is she?"

Rob hesitated for a minute before realizing that he had no cause for embarrassment. Hell, he had a right to a social life. He was normal, wasn't be?

Every bit of rationalization notwithstanding, his grin was a self-conscious one. "She's very attractive."

"She must be. You don't date a helluva lot."

"Her looks aren't why I'm seeing her."

"No? Then it's really serious? Man, you'll shake up the staff here but good!"

"Come on, Howard. Whether or not there's anything serious about it, the woman happens to be intelligent and a pleasure to be with."

"Many women are, but you've never been interested before—at least, not to the point of asking me to cover."

"You're sure you don't mind?"

"Of course I'm sure. Nancy and I were going to be around, anyway. Jonathan's been out of school with a strep infection all week. He won't be up to doing much."

Rob grinned. "Thanks, pal. I really appreciate this."

"My pleasure."

Rob called Heather shortly after noon on Friday. "I'm covered for Sunday. How about if we take off? If you're free, that is." It suddenly occurred to him that he'd taken that small matter for granted when he'd had no right to do so.

Heather didn't mind in the least. "Yes, I'm free, and yes, I'd love to take off. Where will we go?"

"I don't know. For a drive in the country, maybe. Why don't we wing it?"

"I'd like that."

He chuckled. "I've never 'winged it' before. It'll be an adventure. I've always had my life scheduled down to the minute. Something must be happening to me." He'd thought and thought about what he'd want to do with Heather. Traditionally he'd have bought tickets to a show or made reservations at a fine restaurant. Somehow, though, he didn't want to feel traditional with Heather. He simply wanted to be with her.

"If it's any consolation, I've never 'winged it' before, either." She'd never felt carefree enough, but she did now and she loved the feeling. "How about if I pack a picnic—"

"We can stop somewhere. You don't have to—"

"I know I don't have to, but I want to."

He was silent for a moment, thinking of sitting with her in a quiet spot, perhaps by a brook with trees overhead. "That'd be great," he said, his voice deeper than usual. "I'll pick you up at ten?"

"I'll be ready," she said with a broad smile. The smile stayed with her long after she hung up the phone.

HE ARRIVED five minutes early, but she was ready. They drove to South Lyme, parked the car and set out on foot to explore Rocky Neck State Park. Heather's excitement compensated for the fact that she tired fairly quickly, but by the time they were talking about lunch she was more than ready for a rest.

They found a perfect spot for their picnic, a quiet, shaded clearing with a brook trickling nearby. "It's just as I imagined," Rob said. He was unpacking their lunch while Heather sat relaxing against a tree.

"What is?" she asked.

"This spot. When I think of you I think of places like this. Peaceful. Serene. Relaxing." He took a piece of shrimp, dunked it in cocktail sauce and handed it to her.

Heather accepted the shrimp with a smile of thanks. "You do look relaxed." He was wearing a pair of khaki slacks, a dark brown shirt, open at the neck, sleeves rolled up, and loafers. The walk through the woods had added color to his cheeks, and what with the way the breeze had ruffled his hair, he looked decidedly carefree.

"I feel it." He set a loaf of French bread next to the containers of shrimp and sauce on the spread linen, removed the lid from a large bowl of fresh fruit, then poured two glasses of wine and handed her one. Finally he stretched out on his side, propped himself on an elbow and popped a cantaloupe ball into his mouth. "I never imagined I was the picnic type. Or the hiking type, for that matter." He tipped his head back to look at her. "You got a little winded. Feel okay now?"

"Fine. The walking I usually do is more sedate than this, that's all." She steered the subject from herself. "You didn't even work up a sweat. How did you manage it?"

"I'm cool," came his ridiculous drawl.

She couldn't help but laugh as she reached for another shrimp. "You probably also run five miles a day."

"Right. Up one hospital corridor and down the next."

"Seriously, Rob. How do you stay in shape?" She wanted to know what she was up against.

"I exercise every morning at home."

"But when? If you're at the hospital by six . . ."

"At five." He gave a sheepish grin and a shrug. "I'm *really* a morning person."

"What time do you go to bed at night?"

"Eleven . . . twelve. I don't need more than five or six hours' sleep."

"You're lucky. I need a solid eight or I suffer."

"Our bodies are different," he drawled, meaningfully this time.

"Is that so," she countered pertly.

"Uh-huh." He found himself thinking of those differences, looking at them. Clearing his throat, he averted his gaze. "Anyway, I get plenty of exercise in the course of a day, not only up and down corridors, but up and down stairs and from one building to the next. I seem to be forever on the move." He patted his lean stomach. "No chance for rolls to develop."

Her eyes lingered on his stomach. It was perfectly flat, solid. She imagined the way it looked beneath his shirt, a hard span of muscle and flesh. She wondered if there was a line of dark hair bisecting it, wondered how it would feel to the touch, the taste. She sucked in a shaky breath.

"Heather?"

"Hmm?"

A chunk of bread cut off her view of his middle. "Have some," he said, one side of his mouth curving knowingly.

Properly chastised, she accepted the bread and concentrated on regaining her senses while she chewed it.

They ate in companionable silence for a time, sharing the restfulness of the scene. Then Rob spoke in a quiet, almost wistful voice.

"When I was a kid, my parents used to take us on outings like this and I hated it. I just wanted to be back home doing whatever it was I felt had been forcefully interrupted. There was always something that seemed more important. But it's strange. Sitting here now I feel content." Puzzled, he looked up at her. "Why is it we always want to rush through life?"

"Maybe because we're afraid we won't get everything done in time, that life will pass us by while we're out lolling on the grass."

"Do you feel that way?"

"You found me working outside last Sunday, didn't you?"

"But you put the work aside when I got there."

"Being with someone is an activity in itself," she said, but she didn't want to push that issue. "Tell me about your family, Rob. Do your parents still work?"

"My dad's a plastic surgeon. Mom teaches piano."

"No kidding? And your sister and brother?"

"Tom is a professor of economics at the University of Michigan. Vickie sells real estate."

"Are either of them married?"

"Both."

"Children?"

"Tom's get three, Vickie one."

"Do you see them often?"

"Christmas is about the only time we all get together."

"It must be fun."

Rob shrugged.

"No?"

"I feel a little out of it. I guess I always did." He sent her an apologetic look. "I never really was the family-man type. I never went for the noise, or the diapers, or the sticky fingers, or the squabbling."

"But what about the quiet times, times when the diapers were dry and the fingers were clean and the kids were giggling with one another?"

He sighed. "Those times seemed so few and far between. I was always relieved to be able to race back to the hospital.... I must sound terribly callous to you."

"No. I respect your feelings. They're not unique. Many people opt for careers over families."

"It's a shame it has to be one or the other."

"It doesn't have to be. There's middle ground if you look for it."

He thought about that for a minute. "I guess I've never looked."

"It's never too late."

"I don't know, Heather. I'm nearly forty. I've blown what I might have had with my own two children."

"Blown? Is it really irreparable?"

"They're coming up in a couple of weeks. Gail and Charles want to spend some time in Manhattan, so the kids will be staying with me for the weekend. I'm already nervous trying to think up things to do with them. I've got a sitter lined up, a local girl, who can stay with them when I have to be at the hospital."

"Oh, Rob, there are lots of things you can do with them," Heather cried with enthusiasm. "The weather's so gorgeous now—you can take them picnicking like this, or to the beach or a lake. You can take them to the Trolley Museum. I bet they'd even love playing around your yard. Is Michael into baseball?"

"A little."

"So you can throw a ball around with him. Or you could put a tetherball up, or Zim-Zam."

"Zim-Zam?"

"It's like tetherball, but using rackets and a smaller ball. You buy the complete set. All you have to do is stick a pole into the ground, stand the kids on either side with rackets in their hands and see which one can hit the ball enough to wind the rope all the way around the pole."

"What if it rains?"

"You can take them to the Peabody Museum. They're just the right ages to be fascinated by dinosaur skeletons. Or go to a movie."

"I suppose." He tipped his head. "How come you know so much about what to do with kids?"

He'd asked it jokingly, but Heather's expression sobered and her voice grew softer. "Because I spend lots of time dreaming about what I'll do with my own children, if I ever have any."

"Whaddya mean, if you ever have any?" he growled, trying to restore the lighter mood. "You'll have kids. You'd make a wonderful mother." When she remained unconvinced—about what, he wasn't sure—he pushed himself up, nudged her away from the tree so he could lean back, and drew her in to rest against his shoulder. "You would make a wonderful mother. You should be one already."

She shrugged, but if she was aiming to appear indifferent, she failed. Looking down at her, Rob caught the sadness in her eyes.

"What is it?" he prompted gently.

"Nothing."

"Something's upset you. Was it my mentioning your having children?"

"It's nothing. Really." She rubbed her cheek against his chest. She didn't want to think about having or not having children, not when Rob was finally holding her as she'd been aching to be held. "This is nice," she said with a serene smile.

He wanted to prod, to ask more about what had brought on that melancholy look, but he, too, grew absorbed with the moment. Having Heather in his arms felt comfortable. She was so soft and pliant. "It is nice," he agreed.

"Mmm. The reward for exertion."

"All tuckered out?"

"Just feeling lazy. Maybe it's the wine."

He looked down and saw that she'd closed her eyes. "Is it putting you to sleep . . . or am I?"

"A little of each."

"Hmmph."

"That's a compliment. I feel content, too." She took a deep, deep breath, savoring the clean male scent of his body. He didn't use cologne or scented after-shave. He didn't have to. He was alluring enough just the way he was. There was no question in her mind that she'd be happy to stay this way forever. . . .

The next thing she knew she was opening her eyes and something was different. Her position. She was curled on her side with her head in Rob's lap, and he was stroking, ever so gently stroking, her hair. She blinked, forced her eyes wide, turned onto her back so that she could look up at him.

"Oh, no, I fell asleep, didn't I?"

He grinned. "Sure did."

"I'm sorry, Rob! What an awful thing for me to do! Here you've taken me off for the day and I fall asleep on you!"

"I like it when you fall asleep on me. You're very soft." He scooped her up in his arms until her face was inches from his own. "And very tempting." His lips took hers in a hungry caress, and almost instantly she was responding to his kiss. Turning to him, she slid her arms around his neck.

"What you do to me," she whispered when at last her mouth was free.

"Not half of what I'd like," he murmured. He lowered his mouth again, this time sliding one arm diagonally across her back to support her while the other touched her neck, the hollow of her throat, her breasts.

She whimpered involuntarily, feeling so suddenly alive and burning that she would have been frightened had not the greater force of passion overshadowed all else. Threading her fingers into the vibrant hair at his nape, she held his head closer. Her grasp became a lifeline when he tugged her shirt from her jeans and slid his hand over her torso.

"It's okay, honey," he soothed against her lips. "I just need to touch you." Before she could speak, he had the front catch of her bra undone and was gliding his palm over her bare breast.

She didn't want to say a thing then. She couldn't have, anyway. She was too busy absorbing the sensation of her flesh being intimately molded to Robert's hand. Her breasts grew fuller, nipples puckering and straining, until at last his fingers gave her the satisfaction she sought.

Lips pressed to his cheek, she gasped softly, then gasped again when he drew the shirt up until her breasts were open to his gaze. He stared at her for a moment, then lowered his head and opened his mouth over one rosy nipple. He sucked it, tongued it, took it gently between his teeth until incoherent sounds slid from her throat.

"Oh, God, Rob," she uttered brokenly. "Not here!"

"Shhh. We're all by ourselves."

"That's not it," she cried, pulling herself up to face him. Her shirt fell down to cover her breasts, but she didn't notice. She was breathing hard and fast, knowing only that there was a fire burning in her that would surely reduce her to ashes if what he'd started couldn't be consummated. "I want more and we can't do that here."

Driven to boldness by desperation, she dropped her hands to his chest, then lower. Her eyes didn't leave his. She felt his belt beneath her fingers, then the hardness straining against his fly. It was the latter she savored, moving her hands up and down with agonizing slowness.

Rob closed his eyes in the same instant that his hips strained upward. "Where did you learn to do that?" he demanded gruffly.

"Right here. Right now. I want you, and I can feel how much you want me." She looked frantically around. "Isn't there somewhere we can go?"

He put his hand over hers, pressed it tight to his sex for a minute, then determinedly lifted it. "No, honey. Not yet."

"Not yet! Oh, Rob, why not? You're driving me crazy!"

"Maybe that's the point," he said with a wry grimace.

She sat back on her heels. "I don't understand."

"The point is to build it up and build it up until neither of us can stand anymore. Then it'll be absolutely beautiful."

"It wouldn't be beautiful now?"

"Not as beautiful as it will be if we wait."

"You sound like a Victorian maid," she pouted. "I'm the one who should be talking that way."

"And since you're not, it's my responsibility," he said more calmly. Taking both of her hands in his, he kissed her knuckles. "And if you think I won't suffer for it, think again." With a despairing glance down at himself, he pushed himself to his knees, crawled the short distance toward where the remains of their picnic lay and began to clean up.

After a minute, Heather gave him a hand. One part of her admitted he was right. The other part was a mass of frustration. But he was determined. She knew that. And she wouldn't force him to change his mind. Physical want was one thing, emotional want quite another. Right now, she sensed Rob still had some thinking to do about their relationship. She had no fear of making the commitment that lovemaking would entail, but until he was comfortable making it, things would have to stand as they were.

4

Rob came for dinner on Thursday night, then, albeit on call, to spend the day Sunday. The following Wednesday night he took Heather to eat at a local inn, and they went shopping together on Saturday afternoon.

"You've thoroughly enjoyed this, haven't you?" he asked with a good-humored grimace. They were in a snack shop at the shopping mall, with his purchases tucked in bags under the table.

Grinning broadly, Heather was without remorse. "You bet I have. You looked great in all of it."

"I haven't worn jeans in years. I'll probably feel like I'm in a straitjacket."

"Did you feel that way when you tried them on?"

"No . . ."

"See? Things have changed. Jeans are prewashed now, so they're soft, and they fit perfectly."

"You sound like an ad."

"Besides," she chided, ignoring his playful barb, "you can't wear slacks with creases when you're riding a bike."

He put on a scowl, but it was just that—put on—and they both knew it. He'd enjoyed the buying spree as much as she had. "If I'd known you'd con me into getting a whole new wardrobe, I might have thought twice before suggesting the jeans."

"Trust me, Rob," she stated with conviction. "You'll wear everything you bought."

At her urging, he'd picked up, in addition to the jeans, a chambray shirt, several knit pullovers, a summer sweater, a pair of sneakers and a Windbreaker. She hadn't quite had the courage to suggest that he buy a pair of swim trunks; that would have been pushing her luck.

As it was, she was tempting fate by agreeing to go bicycling with him the next day. Years of conditioning had made her hesitant, but she desperately wanted to go— not only because she'd been fantasizing about it for so long, but because Rob had suggested the outing and she knew it was another door opening for him.

So, on Sunday they rented bicycles and pedaled along the Connecticut River. They stopped frequently, when she tired, and though he didn't appear at all suspicious of the cause, Rob was fully solicitous. Nonetheless she was grateful that he left after they'd eaten a light dinner together, because she was asleep on the sofa by eight-thirty. When the phone rang at nine, she answered it groggily.

"Oh-oh. I woke you up."

"No, no. I was just resting," she managed, trying to sound more awake than she felt as she pushed herself up.

"Today really tired you, didn't it? You looked a little peaked when I left."

"I'm fine. Really. And I had a wonderful time. Thanks for taking me, Rob. I never would have done something like that alone."

"Neither would I. It was fun, wasn't it?"

"Mmm."

"Can I see you Wednesday night?"

"Sure. . . . When are Dawn and Michael due?"

"Friday. Gail said she'd drop them at the hospital sometime in the afternoon. That way she and Charles can get into Manhattan in time for dinner and a show."

"Can you take off early?"

"I don't know. Helen has offered to keep an eye on the kids until I'm free."

"You can arrange it, Rob," she urged softly. "Just do a little extra Thursday night. I bet Dawn and Michael would even enjoy following you around the hospital."

"They're kids. It's not the place for them."

"But it'd give them a chance to see what you do. What kid doesn't like to play with a real stethoscope, or a dictaphone, or even go to the coffee shop for a dish of ice cream? Just try to think up light things for them, then plan an hour of your time accordingly. They'll love it."

Rob didn't feel as sure as Heather sounded, but he'd thought a lot about her saying it wasn't too late for him to salvage his relationship with his children. And he trusted her judgment. If she thought they'd enjoy a glimpse of his life, and if he could arrange it and not compromise hospital rules, it was worth a try.

When Heather saw him on Wednesday night, she made a point of not harping on the weekend. She had put the bug in his ear, given him suggestions as to what he could do to entertain the children, but beyond that it wasn't her business. She couldn't intrude on his life. She simply accepted the fact that she wouldn't be seeing him that weekend.

Rob had mixed feelings about the entire arrangement. Not only was he nervous about having the children for two full days, but he was sorry that he wouldn't be seeing Heather. On the one hand he wanted her to get to know the children; on the other he felt that he had to get to know them himself first.

After an inauspicious start, with Gail leaving a subdued Michael and Dawn at the hospital Friday afternoon, things picked up. As Heather had predicted, the children responded to his attempts to please them. In turn he found it wasn't as difficult as he'd thought. He'd never made the effort before, but it seemed that the effort itself, more than anything, was his ace in the hole. Not that the children became his bosom buddies in the course of two days, but at least they seemed to be having fun, which was a huge step forward.

By Sunday midmorning, though, Rob was missing Heather. Knowing that he had until five o'clock before Gail and Charles returned, he put in a call to Chester.

"Rob! I didn't expect to hear from you. Is everything all right?"

"Just fine. But I thought we'd take a ride up and say hello. Are you going to be around?"

Heather's heart started pounding. "Sure. I'll be here."

"Would you mind if we stopped by?"

"I'd love it!" He was going to introduce her to his children. It could mean nothing. On the other hand . . .

"Great. See you soon." He put down the phone, feeling refreshed and excited.

"Where are we going, Daddy?" Michael asked as Rob trundled them into the car.

"We're taking a drive up-country to see a friend of mine. She's got a beautiful old house and a huge yard with lots of trees to climb."

"But there are lots of trees to climb here," Michael argued. He wasn't being exactly negative, though he obviously felt some trepidation.

Dawn, two years older and wiser, wasn't thinking of the "lots of trees to climb." She was thinking of the "friend of mine." "Is she your girlfriend?" she asked, shooting Rob a nervous glance from the passenger's seat.

Michael leaned in from the back seat. "Daddy doesn't have girlfriends."

"How do you know?"

"I know."

"You think you know everything."

"And it's supposed to be my turn in the front seat. You had it last time."

"My legs are longer. Besides, I'm a girl."

"What's that got to do with anything?"

"It's polite to put a girl in the front seat."

"You just dreamed that up. When we're in the car with Mommy and Charles, you sit in back with me."

"I don't have any choice. Who is she, Daddy?"

Rob, who under other circumstances would have been annoyed with the bickering, felt surprisingly calm. "She's a special friend. Her name's Heather Cole."

"Do you date her?"

"Yes."

Dawn shot a smug look back at Michael, but the smugness vanished when she returned her attention to Rob. "Are you going to marry her?"

"I haven't really thought that far."

"Do you love her?"

"I haven't thought that far, either."

Michael rejoined the discussion. "Then why are you taking us to meet her?"

"Because I think you'll enjoy her, and I want her to meet you. She's heard a lot about you."

"She has?" Dawn asked.

Rob nodded.

"Does she have kids of her own?"

"No. She's never been married."

"That doesn't mean anything," Michael informed him. "My friend Christopher hasn't ever had a father."

"Of course he has," Dawn countered scathingly. "He just doesn't know him."

Michael bristled. "His mother never got married."

"But he had to have a father. Don't you know anything about the facts of life?"

Rob slanted her a glance, wondering just how much *she* knew about the facts of life. Most everything, he decided. She was growing up, looking even older than he'd have thought a twelve-year-old would look. She was very pretty, and she was beginning to develop. He wondered if she'd gotten her period yet.

She met his gaze, and for a minute he felt a sense of pride. As though aware of his thoughts, she looked away, pink cheeked.

"You'll both like Heather," he said gently. "She's quiet, but she's got a lot of spirit. She's the one who suggested Zim-Zam."

That seemed to appease both children, since they'd adored the game he'd picked up with them the day before. Nonetheless, both were silent, decidedly shy, when they arrived at Heather's and he introduced them.

"I wanted to show the kids your tree house," Rob said, eyes twinkling. He also wanted to take Heather in his arms and kiss her senseless, but he'd conditioned himself to curb that urge. It wasn't easy, particularly with her looking as sweet as she did in her one-piece, yellow-and-white shorts outfit. She was wearing sandals and a chunky necklace made of brightly colored beads. He couldn't resist touching it. "Did you make this?"

"Uh-huh."

He turned to Dawn, whose eyes were glued to Heather. "Heather is a professional craftswoman. She makes handbags for a living. Maybe later she'll show you her workroom.... Michael? Wait up." He loped off to catch up with Michael, who had wandered away in search of the tree house.

Heather felt nearly as awkward as Dawn looked. "Should we follow them?" she asked quietly. When Dawn nodded, the two started out. "Have you had a nice weekend?"

"Very nice, thank you."

"Done anything interesting?"

"Daddy showed us around the hospital. He's never done that before."

"You're getting older. He can do it now."

"We went to a super Tex-Mex place for dinner Friday night."

"In New Haven?"

"Uh-huh."

"And Saturday?"

"We played around the house in the morning. Daddy had to go to the hospital for a little while, but when he got home we went shopping. We bought Zim-Zam. Thank you for suggesting it."

"Was it fun?"

"I beat Michael five times."

"I bet Michael loved that," Heather speculated, tongue in cheek.

"He's a lousy loser. I let him win a couple. So did Daddy."

"He did, did he?" She was smiling.

"Uh-huh. We also played softball for a while, but I got tired of it, so I went in to read a book. Did you really make that necklace?"

"Sure."

"Is it hard to do?"

"No. Have you ever worked with your hands?"

"I made a lanyard with gimp last year."

"The diamond stitch?"

"Uh-huh. It's not as pretty as that, though."

"Thank you.... Maybe you'd like to make one."

"A necklace like that?"

"I've got the beads and all inside. It doesn't take very long to do."

Dawn wrinkled up her nose. "I probably wouldn't be able to do it very well."

"I'll help you. It's not hard." They'd reached the tree house. Rob, looking slightly dismayed, was standing behind a wide-eyed Michael.

"Maybe this wasn't such a good idea," he said to Heather. "Michael wants to climb it, but it's really pretty unsafe."

Heather shrugged. "There's a lumberyard in town. I think it's open today. You could pick up a few planks and see what progress you can make." Her gaze dropped along the length of his body. "You're dressed for it." He was wearing jeans and one of the knit pullovers he'd bought with her, and he looked utterly virile.

Oblivious to the vibes suddenly passing between the two adults, Michael looked at his father. "Can we?"

Rob tore his gaze from Heather's and rubbed the back of his neck. "Uh, I'm not exactly a carpenter."

"I had woodworking in camp," the boy rushed to assure him. "I know what to do."

"Yeah," Dawn injected dryly. "You should see the bookshelf he brought home."

Michael turned on her indignantly. "There was nothing wrong with it. And look who's talking. Your napkin holder hasn't held a napkin yet."

"That's because Mommy has a Plexiglas one that goes with the rest of the kitchen. At least my napkin holder works."

"So does my bookshelf."

"As long as you anchor things to it so they don't slide off."

"You dip—"

"Okay, okay," Rob interrupted. "Let's not have that." He sent a helpless glance at Heather. "Maybe I will take a ride in town to see what they've got. Come on. Let's go."

"Daddy?" It was Dawn, hanging back when Rob started forward. "Could Heather and I stay here?" Rob looked at Heather, but Dawn was the one who answered his unspoken question. "Heather's going to show me how to make a necklace like hers."

"Oh, sure," Michael sneered, unwilling to let the argument go when he still felt the sting of his sister's insult. "That'll be some necklace."

"It'll be better than one you could make."

"I don't want to make one. I want to fix the tree house." He looked up at Rob. "Let her stay. She'll be in the way if she comes with us."

"No, she won't," Rob countered a second before Heather stepped in, putting a light hand on his arm.

"Why don't you two go ahead," she offered. "Michael would be pretty bored with my workroom, anyway."

"You're sure?"

She nodded. "Dawn and I will keep busy. You two get what you need. I've got a hammer here, but you'd better get nails. And stop at McDonald's."

"McDonald's?"

Heather looked at Dawn. "What'll it be?"

Dawn didn't hesitate. "A quarter-pounder and a small order of fries. And a Coke."

"I'll have the quarter-pounder without the fries and the Coke," Heather said to Rob, whose bemusement was being replaced by a grin. She savored it for a minute, then put her arms around Dawn's shoulder and headed off, calling over her shoulder, "There's a drive-in window. If you stop there on your way home, the food will still be hot when you get back."

Rob shook his head, laughed softly, then turned to his son. "You up for McDonald's?"

"You bet," was Michael's bright response.

"YOU THINK well on your feet," Rob commented when he got Heather on the phone that night. "I wasn't sure what I was going to do with them when I got them to your place, but it all worked out. Gail was already here and waiting when we finally got back."

"Was she angry?"

"How could she be? The kids were happy. Dawn was proud as punch of her necklace, and Michael was full of talk about the tree house."

"How's your thumb?"

"Turning purple. Lucky it's my left one."

"Lucky it wasn't a direct hit."

"Aw, come on. I wasn't that inept. Anyway, Michael seemed to think it was pretty funny. He showed me the scar on his finger where he bobbled the saw blade when he was making his bookshelf."

"Like son, like father...though I think Dawn looks more like you than Michael. They're both beautiful children, Rob. You should be proud of them."

"I am. For the first time, I think I am. Even the fighting wasn't so bad."

"You handled it well. All kids fight. You just have to let it go in one ear and out the other."

Rob was silent for a moment, and when he finally spoke his voice was full of emotion. "Thank you, Heather."

"For what?"

"For being there. For letting us come over. For putting the icing on a really nice weekend."

Happiness spread warmly through her entire body. "My pleasure."

"I hope you know that the next time they come they're going to want to drive up there again."

She nodded. Then realizing he couldn't see her, she said, "I'll look forward to it."

"Can you look forward to dinner on Wednesday night? This is becoming a habit, I think."

"Am I complaining?"

IT WAS WONDERFUL, and yes, habit-forming. Heather enjoyed every minute she spent with Rob, and even those she didn't, because the pleasure of knowing he'd call, the anticipation of seeing him again was satisfying in itself.

Though they'd been comfortable with each other from that very first Sunday when he'd shown up unannounced at her house, they'd become even more so as the weeks passed. Rob learned that Heather lived a fairly structured life, that she cleaned a room a day in the house, that she was rarely awake after ten at night, that she preferred pineapple cottage cheese or yogurt to eggs and rarely ate red meat. Heather learned that Rob liked his tomato juice with a touch of Tabasco sauce, that he took notes on a large yellow pad when he was reading journals, that indeed there were days when he was preoccupied with something or other that had happened at the hospital. On occasion he discussed a particular problem with her. Other times he was silent. But, as she'd promised, she accepted him for what he was, and she was always grateful for his mere presence.

Only two things bothered her as the weeks passed. The first was that, as close as they were, she still hadn't told Rob about her heart condition. She thought about it every night, planned to tell him the next time she saw him, but when that time came she inevitably had an excuse. Either he was too relaxed to be disturbed, or he was worried about something at the hospital and she didn't want to compound that, or she was simply enjoying his company too much to put a wrinkle in her own pleasure. Her guilt grew, though, and she knew that the longer she waited the harder it would be, but she wasn't able to help herself.

The second thing that bothered her was that Rob seemed determined to downplay the chemistry that flared so strongly between them. Oh, he kissed her, and there were times when he lost himself and began to touch her until she cried for more, but he always caught himself before the point of commitment, leaving her breathless and tense with frustration. She could only hope—perversely, perhaps, but she didn't care—that Rob's frustration was as great.

It was. He took cold showers every time he left her, and even began doing push-ups at night—anything to vent the excess energy that burgeoned when he thought of her. His body was more than ready to make love to her, and he was beginning to wonder what he was waiting for. She was special. She was always on his mind. She was delightfully undemanding, indeed understanding of the demands his career made on his life.

What frightened him was the probability that their relationship might change with that act of lovemaking, of commitment.

THAT SUNDAY he picked her up and they drove south toward the beach at Fenwick, where the Connecticut River merged into Long Island Sound.

"You've got your suit on under those?" he asked, taking his eyes from the road long enough to skim her shorts and T-shirt, which had Big Bam Boom plastered on it. He knew enough not to ask what it meant.

"Uh-huh." She eyed his jeans and shirt. "And you?"

"Sure." He tried to make his voice sound nonchalant, but it was hard. The mere thought of seeing Heather in a bikini was affecting his body in ways that would be embarrassing once they were on the beach. "This could be difficult," he mumbled under his breath, but she heard.

"What could?" she asked, sensing precisely what was going to be difficult.

"Keeping myself in control when you're wearing that—" he waved his hand "—that little nothing."

She grinned. It was nice to know she wasn't the only one with a problem. "It's not such a little nothing. I've seen worse."

He grunted, but reached over for her hand and squeezed it.

"Besides," she reasoned, "there'll be lots of people around."

A mixed blessing, he mused. "Did you bring suntan lotion?"

"Uh-huh. And towels."

"Good. I've got lunch, so we should be all set. Did you bring your cassette player?"

"With the sounds of the beach all around? No way. Besides," she said with a smirk, "I doubt you'd take to my music."

"Isn't it awfully...loud?"

"Not when you keep the volume down," she teased, knowing that wasn't what he'd meant. "Howard's covering for you?"

"Yup." He willingly dropped the issue of pop music and sent her a mischievous look. "He's beginning to ask questions."

"About . . . ?"

"You."

"What do you tell him?"

"That you're a mystery lady. But it's only piqued his curiosity. He wants to meet you."

"I'd like that," she said, picturing an evening with Howard and his wife and, of course, Rob. She and Rob hadn't done anything with other people yet. It would be a further step in their relationship, going public, so to speak.

"Maybe you'll come in to the hospital one day. Helen's anxious to meet you, too."

Heartbeat faltering, Heather simply smiled and nodded. Going in to the hospital was something she hadn't counted on. The hospital gave her the willies. It was one thing for Rob to tell her about it; she felt somehow removed hearing him talk on nameless cases. But to be there, to remember the reason she'd originally sought him out—she wasn't sure she was comfortable with that idea. Not just yet. Not just yet.

Fortunately her mind was diverted as soon as they reached the beach, though another kind of tension set in then, a delicious one, an agonizing one. It began when they'd laid their towels out and the moment of stripping arrived. Rob looked at her; she looked at him.

"You first," he said, falling to his knees on his towel. "You're the one who's used to the beach."

She knelt, too, and shook her head. "You first. You already know what my bathing suit looks like."

"Mine's navy. Now you know." He gave a toss of his chin. "Come on. Ladies before gentlemen."

"Chivalry's a little outmoded. These are modern times."

"How about we do it together?"

The delay was only making it worse. "Sounds fair." Without further word she crossed her arms, reached for the hem of her T-shirt and whipped it over her head. By the time she'd emerged, Rob's chest was bare and, evidently agreeing with her lest-I-lose-courage haste, he was reaching for the snap of his jeans. Her heart skipped far more than a beat. Her mouth went dry. She quickly looked down, but even under her scrutiny her fingers couldn't seem to slide smoothly beneath the waistband of her shorts. At last she managed to push the cotton fabric to her thighs. Then she sat back with a thud and freed her legs.

When she looked up again, Rob was staring at her—her face, then her shoulders, then her breasts, then her very bare middle, then the swatch of fabric below, then her thighs. His visual examination was nearly tangible. Moistening her lips, she began one of her own, following the course he'd taken but over hard male contours rather than softer female ones. Everything she'd imagined was there and then some—broad shoulders, hair-roughened chest, narrow waist, lean hips, strong thighs. She swallowed hard and tried to catch her runaway pulse as she met his gaze.

He was no more than an arm's length away, and his voice was slightly strangled. "I'm not sure I'm going to make it."

"You're not the only one."

"You're beautiful."

"So're you."

"Maybe this wasn't such a good idea."

"The damage is already done."

"Right.... So what do we do now?"

"We either lie down in the sun, take a walk on the sand, or go in the water."

"I vote for water."

"Smart move."

He was up and taking her hand nearly before her words were out, and they ran toward the waves, through the waves, over the waves, then dived. When Heather came up, she was as breathless as she'd ever remembered being. Frantically she looked around for Rob, only to find that he was stroking quickly away from shore. She thought to call out, but he wouldn't hear her and she didn't want to alarm him. So she took a step back and stood with the water on a level with her breasts, taking deep breaths, willing her heart to calm down.

"Hey!" Rob called, waving from a distance then heading back toward her. When he reached her, he whipped his head around to shake his hair free of water, then stood. "That was great!" He was wearing a wide grin, but it faded almost instantly and he reached for her arms. "What's wrong, honey? You look like you've seen a ghost."

With his return, her heart seemed to have regained a saner beat. "I haven't been swimming, really swimming in so . . . long that I guess the water took me by surprise. I lost . . . my breath for a minute. I'm okay now."

"Are you sure?"

She smiled and nodded vigorously. The ocean lapped against her chest.

"God, you look gorgeous," he breathed. His eyes skipped over her hair, which streamed back wet and gleaming in the sun, just as he'd imagined. Aided by the water, he lifted her against him and kissed her. But her fingers grew tight on his shoulders and she dragged her mouth away.

"Let me catch my breath," she panted, and it seemed the most natural thing that her head should fall to his exposed shoulder while, beneath the waves, her legs should float up to wind around his waist.

"Take all the time you want," he murmured in a singsong tone. "I'm in heaven."

"You're awful," she teased, but she was suddenly in the same heaven. His hands were cupping her bottom, and the intimate fit of their bodies felt so very right that she didn't care how breathless she was as long as she could stay this way.

"Better?" he asked, riding up with a wave, then settling.

"Better."

"Want to swim now?"

"Not just yet."

"Want to stay like this a little longer?"

"Mmm." Another wave took them up, then down. "You're strong. I feel secure with you."

"You make me feel strong . . . as if I could take on the world and conquer it."

"You're already doing your share."

"But you've broadened that, or hadn't you noticed?"

Arms clasped about his neck, she raised her head. "You're making time for yourself."

"For us," he corrected, his eyes holding hers. "Maybe that's the difference. It wouldn't occur to me to do the things alone that I've done with you. They wouldn't be fun alone. You give meaning to them."

Heather felt her heart swell at his words, then constrict at the words she wanted to say. *I love you.* They came into her mind from nowhere, but she had no doubt as to their truth.

And she didn't dare utter them aloud.

Shaken, she tucked her head back against his neck and clung to him. Before long he began walking toward the shore, setting her down when the water was at waist height, holding her hand as they returned to their towels.

Heather heard none of the playful sounds around her that day. When she closed her eyes, she thought of what she'd learned about herself, and felt confused and worried. When she opened her eyes, she saw Rob lying beside her, his body long and well formed, sun glistening off his skin and the soft, dark hairs that spattered it. She was tormented and tantalized, frightened and aroused, torn and inflamed. By the time they were back in Rob's car at day's end, the inner skirmish she'd waged had taken its toll. She slept most of the way back to Chester, awakening only when Rob very gently touched her arm.

"We're here," he murmured as she opened her eyes.

She looked around, disoriented for a minute. Then her dilemma hit her afresh, and her eyes widened. "I...uh...I didn't mean to fall asleep."

"It's okay. The sun's draining."

"Will you come in?"

"Are you up to it?"

"Sure." She shifted in her seat. "I feel pretty grubby, though, between salt and sand and suntan lotion. I think I could use a shower. Do you want one?"

"That would be nice."

Nodding, she reached for the door handle. By the time she'd climbed from the car, Rob was at her side, tugging the beach bag from the back seat, then, with a hand at her elbow, guiding her up the walk.

At his insistence, she showered first. Mind befuddled, she hadn't thought to bring fresh clothes into the bathroom, so she simply grabbed her thick terry robe from its hook behind the door, put it on and sashed it tightly at the waist. When Rob took her place in the bathroom, she hurried to the kitchen, intent on making a pitcher of iced tea, then dressing before he was done.

He was faster than she'd expected.

She was in the process of refilling the ice trays, when she felt long arms slide around her waist. She jumped, dropped the trays in the sink and gulped in a breath.

"Rob! You frightened me!"

"Who did you think it was?" he teased softly.

"I...no one. I didn't expect anyone. I thought you were still in the shower." She would have heard the water turn off if she'd been paying attention. But her mind had been embroiled in the battle it had been fighting all day.

His lips were warm and moist at her neck then. Covering one of his hands with hers, she closed her eyes. Slowly the battle waned. If he was going to take her away from the torment, she couldn't resist. She wanted him—selfishly, perhaps, but desperately. The sensuality of the day, those moments when she'd looked at him, surged to the fore, and she felt an intense hunger. She saw him again sprawled on the towel, his back corded, his buttocks tight, his legs long, so long and spattered with hair. She saw him turn over, and his front was as devastating. And she felt his bodily warmth, then, now, burning into her skin, spreading fire through her veins.

His mouth was moving along the slender column of her neck, pressing kisses from earlobe to shoulder. She tipped her head in encouragement, ran her hands along forearms, textured and strong, then sighed as the last of her tension broke and dissipated. A sense of euphoria filled her then, washing all thoughts from her mind but those of security, of pleasure.

When Rob turned her in his arms, though, she couldn't help but catch her breath. His chest was bare. His legs were bare. All he wore was a damp towel hooked low around his hips.

"I've tried," was his husky murmur against her forehead, "I've tried to stay away from you, Heather, but I can't. I put off going to the beach because I knew I'd crumble, but maybe that was what I wanted. Seeing you there, with so little covering your body—it was all I could do not to touch you and hold you. All day I've been wanting this. God help me, I can't fight it anymore."

"I know," she whispered, her eyes riveted to his chest. She spread her hands there, drew them slowly over his tapering torso. His flesh was warm, still damp from his shower, and the faint scent of soap joined with a very masculine one to assail her senses in but another way. "I know," she whispered again, unconsciously this time. Her fingers were gently exploring the furry swirls of his upper chest, circling flat, dark nipples, falling along a narrowing trail of hair to his navel.

The muscles of his stomach contracted and his breathing faltered as he fought for control. His need was great, his sex erect against her belly, and if he didn't watch himself he'd be taking her then and there. But she was a virgin. He reminded himself of that over and over again, and it took reminding, because the way she was touching him was anything but virginal.

Framing her face with firm hands, he turned it up and vented his hunger on her lips. He thrust his tongue forward, needing to conquer that which was momentarily at his disposal.

But his need only increased with that minor slaking, and, lips still imprisoning hers, he lifted her in his arms and carried her from the kitchen, through the hall, up the winding staircase to her bedroom.

Heather felt the quilt beneath her back, and a live wire of excitement sizzled through her. This was right. Oh, yes, this was right. She knew it in her mind and her heart, just as her body had known it for days. Robert McCrae was the man for her. She'd never been as sure of anything in her life.

Releasing her mouth, he settled his body half over hers and spread deep kisses over her neck and throat. He felt her hands on his back, moving steadily, kneading skin and muscle, expressing both pleasure and desire without words.

But, then, words had been unnecessary from the start. He remembered seeing her that first day in the hospital corridor, catching her eye. He'd thought at the time that he'd been simply curious, but there had to have been more even then. He'd felt something elemental, and the feeling had only deepened as he'd gotten to know her. She was warm and giving, as precious a woman as he'd ever met. She'd gotten under his skin, become a vital part of his existence. He couldn't deny it any longer.

"Heather . . . Heather . . ." Her name was a whispered homage on his lips, his breath hot against her throat. He slid to her side, leaving one leg over hers, and held himself on an elbow as he sought her gaze. "Heather?"

Breathing shallowly, she managed to raise her lids. They were heavy, and her eyes were glazed with desire. He had his hand at her throat, stroking it gently, moving lower by increments until he'd reached the spot where her lapels crossed.

He was studying her intently, his gray eyes deeper than she'd ever seen them, and for a split second she misinterpreted that depth and panicked. "Don't stop!" she cried on a fragment of breath. "Don't stop now!"

"I won't, honey. I can't. I just want to make sure you're not afraid."

Afraid? She was terrified! She was also throbbing with need, and she was desperately in love.

"I need you, Rob," she whispered, arching off the bed in her body's demand for the hardness, the boldness of his.

But he pressed her gently down again, and his hands went to the sash at her waist. His fingers were unsteady, his voice husky. "I need you, too, but we'll take it slow. I want you to tell me if anything I do bothers you. Okay?"

She could only swallow and nod, because the sash was undone and anticipation prevented her from speaking.

With exquisite care he spread the thick terry cloth to either side, then looked slowly down her naked body, taking in every bit of her with a focus on those parts her bikini had hidden. His hand curved around her thigh and inched up over her hips and her ribs until it fitted the underside of her breast.

Heather watched him as he followed the course of his hand, and her cheeks grew pinker. She was trembling all over, and try as she might she couldn't stop.

"Your body is perfect," he whispered hoarsely.

She didn't even think to argue, because that one imperfection, obvious only to her, was the farthest thing from her mind.

"I'm going to touch you all over," he said as his hand began to move. The arm that propped him up was quivering under the pressure of restraint, but there was such delight in the leisurely exploration of all he'd dreamed about that the restraint was reinforced.

His large palm smoothed over the ivory skin of her breasts, first one, then the other. He watched her nipples bead, and touched their peaks with his fingertips.

She grasped his wrist and drew it away. "My God, Rob!" she cried breathlessly.

"Did that hurt?"

"Pain . . . pleasure . . . I don't know!"

"It's new. That's all. That's the way it's supposed to be." He brushed dots of perspiration from her forehead. "Take a deep, deep breath." She did. Her heart was thudding recklessly. "Now another." She took the second.

He lowered his head and she saw him open his mouth and envelop one taut nipple. She dug her fingers into his damp hair, but she didn't pull him away, because pleasure surmounted pain. He lifted his mouth and she would have cried out at the loss had not his tongue emerged and begun to lave the swollen tip, wetly soothing it even as the subtle rolling action pulled at her womb.

While he adored her breast thus, his hand resumed its exploration of her body, roaming at will, sensitizing her skin in spots she hadn't dreamed could be sensitized. Her body was throbbing by the time he lowered his hand to her thigh. When he began to caress her with an ever higher bent, her muscles tightened.

The focus of her energy was suddenly centered on that spot between her legs. When his hand touched it, she cried out—in surprise, trepidation, fever, she didn't know which or whether it was a combination of the three.

"Shhh. It's okay. I want to touch you there, too," he murmured throatily.

"I feel as if I'm on fire!" was her whispered cry.

"That's how you're supposed to feel, and I'm the only one who can quench the flames." He'd begun to stroke her, but she pressed her thighs together. "Relax, honey. I won't hurt you."

"I know," she gasped. "But it's so new."

"Do you trust me?"

Her yes was short and high.

"Then let me show you what it's like.... Kiss me, Heather," he urged against her lips, then opened his and devoured her at the same time he pressed his knee between her thighs.

His hand returned to its target, and Heather was too caught up in the pleasurable sensations rocketing through her body to object. With a will of their own her thighs fell farther apart, though her muscles had begun to strain toward a new goal. No longer did she seek to hold Rob away. Suddenly she wanted him closer, deeper, harder.

Finely tuned to her need and his own, he gave her what they both wanted. His fingers stroked her, opened her, sought ever deeper haven in a rhythm that was age-old and electrifying. She was panting softly, whimpering from time to time, arching against his hand with untutored knowledge of where salvation lay.

When she felt his fingers deep inside her, she cried out again. "Oh, Rob, it's so . . . so . . . I feel I . . . might burst apart. . . ."

"That's right. It's good. Let it happen, honey."

She was holding to him for dear life, fingers digging into his back. "But I don't know . . . I've never . . ."

"Let go. Trust me and let go."

Suddenly she had no choice. Her body stiffened. The wave of sensation that built beneath his ministration crested, and she was thrown into a blinding paroxysm of bliss.

For a minute she thought she'd died. Then she heard her own helpless gasping and felt the tapering pulsation deep inside her, and she realized what had happened.

Holding Rob tighter, she buried her face against his shoulder and rode out the storm until at last the thundering of her heart began to abate.

She heard something else then, the slow rumbling of a very deep, very masculine, very smug and satisfied chuckle.

"Rob . . . ?"

"That felt so good," he breathed through an audible smile. He was hugging her as tightly as she was him.

"But you . . . didn't feel . . ."

He held her back and gazed into her flushed face. "I felt something I've never before felt, and it was unbelievably beautiful. I love you, Heather. God help me, but I do!"

Heather heard his words, saw them blazing from his eyes, and she did something she hadn't done in years and years. She burst into tears.

5

ROBERT'S EYES went wide in dismay. The raw pain on Heather's face told him her tears weren't ones of happiness. "Heather?"

Sobbing, she pulled away and sat up, burying her face in her hands.

Then, perplexed and frightened, he was sitting, too, squeezing her shoulders, rubbing her arms. "Don't cry. My God, Heather, what's wrong? Is it so terrible that I love you?"

"Yes!"

"But why? Don't you love me?"

"Yes!"

"Then we should be celebrating!"

"But you can't...can't love me! You shouldn't love...me! I'm not...what you think!" She tried to twist from his grasp, but he only tightened it.

"That's impossible," he said with a calm he didn't feel. A niggling idea was beginning to form in the back of his mind. He tried to push it away, but it persisted. "You're warm and soft and sweet and honest—"

She shook her head. "I'm not! I haven't told you. I should have. I kept telling myself to." The phrases came in short clips. Her heart was palpitating wildly, and she couldn't seem to catch her breath.

Rob felt a tightening in the vicinity of his own heart, along with a deep sense of foreboding. He had to fight to keep his voice low, his hands steady as he overcame Heather's resistance and drew her to his chest.

"Shhh. Calm down, honey. Relax first, then you'll tell me whatever it is you should have said."

Her voice was muffled in her hands, which were pressed between her face and his chest. Such a short time before she'd found delight in his near naked body. Now she was oblivious to it. "I'm sorry...it's my fault...I had no right . . . you deserve so much . . ."

"Shhhh." He palmed slow circles over her back. "Shhhh. It can't be all that bad." At least, that was what he was trying to convince himself of, though the muscles of his stomach had coiled into a hard knot and the warmth of the room couldn't dissipate the chill seeping through his limbs.

Heather cried for several more minutes before her sobs gradually subsided. She felt thoroughly flat and weak, as though she'd been through a wringer.

"There," Rob murmured. "That's better." The moment he said the words, he wondered why he had. She was slumped lifelessly against him. The premonition grew stronger. "Now." He kissed the top of her head. "Tell me your deep, dark secret."

A bit of life returned when she began to cry again. He held her upright, cupped her quivering chin in his hand, forced her face up and spoke sternly. He couldn't help himself. "Tell me, Heather. I need to know."

His features were a blur through her tears, but perhaps that was good. At least momentarily, she was able to think of him more abstractly, rather than as the man she so dearly loved. "I have a heart condition. Mitral valve stenosis."

Rob went perfectly still, every bit of the sun's color draining from his face. "What?"

"Mi . . . mitral stenosis."

He stared at her as though she'd spoken a foreign language, rather than one that was second nature to him. "You have mitral stenosis," he echoed dully.

"You know what it is."

"Of course I know what it is." And suddenly the pieces fell together. Breathlessness . . . fatigue . . . quiet lifestyle . . . carefully controlled diet. "That was what brought you to the hospital in the first place, wasn't it?" He released her so quickly that she nearly fell back on the bed. He was staring at the quilt, raking a hand through his hair. "I should have seen it, should have guessed it. The signs were all there, right in front of my nose." He pushed himself from the bed, paced across the room, then turned, eyes flitting blindly from one spot on the floor to another. "I didn't want to see, damn it," he muttered in self-reproach. "I didn't *want* to know what it was you were hiding."

Clutching her robe together, Heather eyed him fearfully. "It was my fault, Rob, not yours. I should have told you that first day—"

"Why didn't you?" His eyes were suddenly large and as demanding as his voice.

She felt a modicum of strength returning to her limbs. Yes, she was upset, and confused, and afraid. But she was also relieved that at last she'd shared the burden. She didn't fully understand what Rob was feeling at that moment, but not once did her trust in him falter.

"I went to that conference because I'd read about you. I knew you were a specialist and I wanted to hear what you had to say. After you'd spoken, I was almost sorry I'd come. You sounded very positive, but there was still so much that scared me. I was torn, as I've been for years, wanting to do things, then not wanting to."

"Things?"

"Things . . . like having an operation to correct the condition."

He took a deep, slightly unsteady breath. "Exactly how bad is it?"

She made a dismissive wiggle of her hand. "Not very bad."

Not very bad . . . yet she'd mentioned an operation. Rob had enough experience with patients to recognize a possible case of denial. "How bad?"

"It's under control." She raked her teeth over her lower lip. "I take care of myself. I limit my intake of salt, make sure I get plenty of sleep, avoid stress. I take penicillin whenever I have dental work done—that's the only risk of infection I've had for years."

"How many?" When she frowned in confusion, he elaborated. "How many years have you suffered from this?"

"I had rheumatic fever when I was nine. We learned about it soon after that."

She hadn't traveled. She hadn't gone swimming . . . or been on a bicycle. She'd been encouraged to take up crafts. Sedate. Quiet. Physically undemanding. "Your parents coddled you."

Heather hesitated. Her breathing was broken by sporadic hiccups, a legacy of her tears. "I suppose you could call it that." She tucked the robe more securely around her and looked away. "They were worried to the point of near panic. I was their only child and they put all their energy into making sure I didn't exert myself. I hated it sometimes. I couldn't do things that the other kids did, things I'd always loved. But I was afraid to break the rules for fear something would happen. As long as I did everything I was supposed to, I felt fine."

"Do you see a doctor regularly?"

"Yes."

He knew all to well that mitral valve disease was progressive. She was still holding back. "Has your condition worsened?"

She couldn't face him. "No. Well...I'm not sure. I don't feel comfortable with the doctor I've been seeing, so I don't ask too many questions. He doesn't say much. He seems satisfied."

"But something brought you to the hospital that day. Something must have been bothering you."

It was harder to explain this part because it dealt with the future, with change and risk. "Nothing physical. But I ... I'd been thinking about it for a while ... about having the operation." The last was said in a near whisper, but Rob heard.

"Is that what your doctor recommended?"

"Not recommended ... exactly."

"Then what?" he prodded quietly.

"When I first learned I had this condition, the doctor—it was our family doctor then and I liked him—said that if I watched myself I could go for years without any problem. He also said, though—" her voice grew smaller

"—that I should plan to have corrective surgery before I considered becoming pregnant."

Rob forced himself to take another deep breath. "Is that what you're considering?"

"Becoming pregnant?" She shrugged, eyes on her fingers, which fidgeted nervously with the sash of her robe. "I'm not getting any younger, and I do want children."

"You need a husband first."

Her eyes flew to his then, pleading for his understanding. "But I've avoided that. I've never openly looked for a husband. One part of me was always frightened of how a man would take the news. I felt I had to do something about the valve business first, come to terms with it somehow or other. Maybe I put the cart before the horse. I don't know." She caught a new breath and raced on. "And I didn't plan for any of this to happen between us. You have to believe that, Rob. I didn't plan to fall in love with you or—" her voice cracked "—or have you fall in love with me."

Rob couldn't be indifferent to either her condition or her plea. Yes, he was feeling impatience, frustration, even anger, but at life's injustices, not at her.

He gentled his voice. "Why did you let it go on so long? Why didn't you tell me sooner?"

"Because I was happy!" she cried. "For the first time in my life, I was really happy! I didn't want to spoil it. Don't you see? I'd never felt this way before. It occurred to me that maybe I was using you, because you were a doctor and you'd be able to take care of me if something happened when we were together. But then there was so much more! I enjoyed your company. You're bright and stimulating. I felt excited when I was with you and I loved looking forward to when we'd be together again. I could forget that you were a doctor, forget that I had a heart condition. I could pretend that everything was natural and normal . . . and it was."

She sagged in defeat, straightening a shaky arm against the bed. "Well, almost. I've been feeling more and more guilty lately. Each time you left me, I swore to myself that I'd tell you everything the next time I saw you. But when that time came, I just couldn't do it." Her eyes filled up and tears began trickling down her already streaked cheeks. "Now it's all spoiled. You know I've got a problem, and I know you don't want the responsibility."

Hearing her words, seeing her tears, feeling the melting sensation in the pit of his stomach, Rob suddenly realized where he was standing. Across the room. Not where he wanted to be.

In three strides he reached the bed. He knelt on it and took Heather in his arms. She went, limply, bleakly.

"I love you, Heather. More than *anything* I want the responsibility."

"But you didn't," she argued against his cheek. "Your life is your work. You told me so. You said you couldn't promise anything. You are what you are. That was what you said."

"That was then, before I fell in love with you—"

"But you didn't know what you were falling in love with!"

He gave a ghost of a laugh. "You sound as if you're some kind of freak. But you're not, Heather. I should know. I deal with problems like yours day in and day out."

"Which is another reason why you shouldn't have to deal with it on your time off."

"To the contrary. You're right. I *am* a doctor and I *do* know what to do if anything happens. I love you. And I'm damn glad it's me you love. I'm not sure I'd trust any other man with your care."

"It's a burden . . . this thing I have."

"No, it's not. Don't get me wrong—I wish to God you didn't have any problem. But you do. It's a fact, and I can't turn my back on it."

"Because of the oath you took."

"Because of the love I feel. I didn't ask for that love, Heather. It hit me between the eyes. I fell in love with you—I told you I loved you—before I even knew about your problem. That love hasn't lessened. It couldn't. If anything it's deepened with the knowledge that you trust me enough to tell me everything." A moment's trepidation gave him pause. "You have, haven't you?"

She looked sharply up. "Isn't it enough?"

"It's not so bad. And it certainly doesn't frighten me. It concerns me, yes. It makes me want to wisk you right over to the hospital to find out the extent of the problem. But I *know* about mitral stenosis, honey. It's nowhere near as serious as many of the things I see. You can't blow it out of proportion."

"It's my life, so it's hard to keep it in proportion!" she exclaimed. But she knew he was right and that she was only exaggerating to let off steam, so she forced herself to calm down. "I've been pretty good. I've made it for twenty years without a major incident. I've adapted to it, and it's not that I spend hours upon hours brooding."

"If that had been the case, you'd have had high blood pressure," he teased.

"I know. I do manage to push it out of my mind." She dropped her gaze. "It's just . . . just that lately it's harder. I've felt so confused. Afraid. Like time's running out."

"Not on your life. Assuming you're stabilized, you can go on this way for a good long time."

"But I want more, Rob. At least, at times I do. I want a husband and I want children, but I can't foist all this on them."

"Once the operation's done, there'll be nothing to foist on anyone. You can lead the normal life you've always wanted."

She raised her head. "Can you be sure, absolutely sure? I heard you quote statistics, and they were optimistic, but there are always failures."

"Nothing's one hundred percent in life, whether it's health or wealth or happiness."

"Can I take that chance? Can you take that chance?"

"It doesn't turn me off, if that's what's got you worried."

"You don't deserve this."

"I don't deserve you. You're too good, too giving." He held her back, his large hands angling her face up for his adoration. "You haven't been the only one to benefit from our relationship. In less than two months you've taught me things about myself I'd never have known. You've opened doors and I've walked through, and I've begun to open them myself. You've shown me that there can be life beyond my work. You've given me reason to seek it out. You don't screech if I'm late getting here, or demand that I come earlier or more often. For the first time I don't quail when I think of my children, thanks to you. You've got me sitting on the grass on a fine summer's day, hiking through the woods, riding a bicycle, swimming in the ocean. Hell, you've even got me wearing dungarees."

"Jeans," she whispered, lips puckering at the corners. "They're called jeans."

"Whatever." He gave her head a gentle shake. "But don't you see? You've given me so much, and you've got so much more to give—in some ways it pleases me that with the medical knowledge I have I can give something back to you."

"You do give something back to me. Lots of things. You call me, you spend time with me, you take me places and have me doing things I wouldn't otherwise do."

"You could have done those things all along, y'know. Within reason, of course."

"But I never felt confident enough. And I never had someone to do them with. You're a special friend—"

"With a capital 'F'?"

She grinned sheepishly. "Yes, with a capital 'F.' You make me feel happy, and special. You give my life focus."

"You had that long before you met me."

"Not the kind of focus I mean. Not the kind I need." She faltered, still feeling she had to make herself clear. "I don't want to use you, Rob."

His hands fell to gently knead her shoulders. "Don't we use each other? Isn't that part of the human condition? Sure, there's a negative side, when a person takes and takes without giving in return. But the positive side entails give and take, sometimes equally, sometimes not, but always with good intent. We do that, Heather. We do it to and for each other. God only knows I've taken enough from you. If I've got something to offer now, I want you to take it."

"But I want you to know that I didn't plan it that way. What's happened since we met boggles my mind. I went to the hospital that first day strictly out of medical curiosity. I didn't know anything about you personally. I pictured you to be bald and portly, with a wife and kids at home. If I'd known you were single and attractive, I'd have probably run in the opposite direction."

His eyes twinkled. "You did just that, as I recall. Even before you knew I was single. My looks must have scared you but good."

"I love your looks," she whispered, taking them in, really seeing them for the first time since she'd burst into tears. "Maybe you did scare me. Maybe I was attracted to you way back then, and even intimidated, but if so I wasn't aware of it. At the time I was only thinking about my heart condition. I didn't want to let you know who I was and what was wrong with me because I felt you'd expect me to follow up with an appointment, and I didn't want that kind of expectation hanging over my head. I was afraid of committing myself medically.... I still am."

Rob wasn't sure he liked her hesitance, but he sensed there was a right way and a wrong way to approach it. "You've been all alone with it, haven't you?" She waited a minute, then nodded. "You haven't told any of your friends about it because you thought they'd think less of you."

"Not less. Just differently. I've had enough of my parents' pitying glances to last me a lifetime. I don't want that from any of my friends. Or from you."

"You won't get pity from me.... I don't spare it for people who don't need it. There's nothing wrong with you that can't be easily fixed." When he saw she was about to argue, he hurried on. "But the point is that you have me now. We can discuss the possibilities together."

"I'm scared, Rob."

"Of me?"

"Of the possibilities."

"No one's going to force you into anything, honey. In the end you have the final say. I would like you to come into the office, though. Before we can outline the possibilities, I'll have to know your state of stenosis."

"But I've been fine. Really I have."

"True. You weathered the hiking and the biking and the swimming with only some minor breathlessness and fatigue. Any intense palpitations?"

"Only a little while ago, when you . . ." Bright color rose on her cheeks and she couldn't finish.

He chuckled. "That's healthy. How about faintness?"

Her voice was little more than a whisper. "Only a little while ago."

This time he hugged her, pressing her head to his chest to absorb her embarrassment. "Did it feel good?"

"Yes."

He squeezed her tighter. "I'm glad. I wanted it to."

Heather took a deep breath, let it out in a sigh, then inhaled again. This time she was aware of his scent, his warmth, his state of undress. She was aware of the fact that she loved him, that he loved her, and that in spite of the turmoil she'd just been through, she was suddenly happy. "Rob?"

"Mmm?"

"Will you . . . will you make love to me, really make love to me?"

"Now? No."

She raised her head. "Why not?"

"Because you've had enough for one day."

Her happiness faded. Abruptly she pushed herself away. "Then you're doing it already. You're treating me differently now that you know."

Undaunted, he shook his head. "Uh-uh. I was treating you differently even before I knew. You *are* different, honey. You're beautiful and innocent and I love you too much to rush you."

"Rush me? I'm the one who's been practically begging, while you act like the vestal virgin!"

He laughed. "Then I guess you'll just have to put my prim mind at ease and marry me."

Heather stared at him, then swallowed. For an instant time stood still. "Marry you?" Her voice was a tiny fragment of sound.

"As in exchange vows and rings and kisses . . ."

She swallowed again, then raised a hand to her head. "I never dreamed . . . I didn't . . ."

"Do you love me?"

"Yes."

"And I love you. So let's get married."

"Uh...I don't know, Rob...things have happened so fast . . ."

"Some of the best things happen that way."

"But maybe they shouldn't. Maybe we should be sure."

"Sure that we love each other? I'm sure. Aren't you?"

"Yes . . . but marriage . . . that's something else. You've already been through an unhappy one. How can you know this would be any better?"

"I can't know, but I can certainly feel and believe. You're different from Gail. The things I feel for you are different from what I felt for her. I'm different from how I was then. I know I'm older. I'd also like to think I'm wiser."

"But to rush into marriage after knowing each other, really, for only a month—"

"It's been the best month of my life. Not perfect, mind you. It would have been perfect if I'd been able to come home to you every night."

"Two days a week. That's all we've had."

His expression grew solemn. "It's not that much less than we'd have if we were married, but there'd be the nighttimes and the part of Saturday when I wasn't working. I warned you about that at the start. You said it wouldn't bother you."

"It wouldn't! It's just . . . how can you think marriage when . . . when we've had so little time together? How can you really know me?"

"What was it you said once—that it was quality, rather than quantity that mattered? The time we've spent together hasn't been spent in theaters or at concerts or crowded parties. We haven't simply accompanied each other places. We've done things with each other. We've interacted. We've talked. You know where I come from, and I know where you come from. Now that I know about your heart condition I can understand even more."

"Such as . . . ?"

"Your respect for medicine. You may not trust it fully, but you take it seriously. Maybe that's why you can put up with my work hours. You appreciate what I do as another person might not." He raised a brow. "I can also see that you've deprived yourself of many of the pleasures in life because you were afraid to indulge."

"I do have to be careful."

"To some extent, yes, but I doubt to the extent you have been. Look at what you've done with me. You've been on a bicycle, which you haven't done in years. You've gone swimming."

"I didn't swim much."

"But you did some, which is more than you've done for, what, twenty years? And you survived."

"If you'd known about my heart condition before, you probably wouldn't have let me do those things."

"Don't assume what I would or would not let you do," he warned, but gently. "I firmly believe that any activity is fine for a woman in your position, as long as common sense is used. Okay, in hindsight I might not have pushed you with the hiking. But that doesn't mean we wouldn't have done it, just that we would have bitten off a smaller piece. The same holds true for bicycling. And don't call it pampering. It's not. It's common sense. And it's something we won't even have to think about once you've had that operation."

The thought of the operation sent chills down Heather's spine. Extricating herself from Rob's light grasp, she slid across the bed and walked to the window. He watched her go, wanting to hold her near but respecting her need for the small distance.

He refused to let her off the hook completely, though. "We've gotten away from the immediate question of when to get married."

"The question was whether to get married."

"No. We'll be married. It's just a matter of now . . . or later."

She was silent for a while, her back to him, her arms wrapped around her waist. "When you came to pick me up this morning, had you planned to ask me to marry you?"

"I didn't plan any of what's happened."

"Then the thought came to you just now?"

"The words came to me just now. I suppose that indirectly I've been thinking about marriage for days."

"How can you think about it 'indirectly'?"

"You can realize that you love someone, that the two of you are totally compatible, that you want to be with her every possible minute, now and in the future."

"You've really thought that all out?"

"I know that I mean all of it. I feel it, Heather. We're right for each other."

"You hate my music."

"You keep the volume down."

"I haven't even seen where you live!"

"That can be easily remedied."

"But . . . but what about Michael and Dawn? You're just beginning to build a relationship with them. Your getting married all of a sudden is bound to upset them."

"Why should it? Their mother remarried fast enough, and I play only a very minor role in their lives."

"That could change. As they get older they might want to spend more time with you."

"They might. But they wouldn't be threatened by our marriage, not after meeting you last weekend. They think you're great." He smiled crookedly. "A lot looser than their old, stuffy dad."

"Then you want to marry me for your kids' sake."

He rose from the bed. "I want to marry you for my sake. And yours."

"You feel sorry for me."

He approached her slowly. "I do not feel sorry for you."

"You're being impulsive. It's not like you. It doesn't make sense."

"What doesn't make sense is why you're hemming and hawing," Rob argued. He was directly before her, his eyes sharp. "What is it, Heather? Are you the one who's afraid of making a commitment to marriage?"

"I've never been afraid of that," she whispered. He towered over her, primitive and bare save the towel at his hips. She realized that he could be intimidating both physically and emotionally...particularly when she was doing little more than grasping at straws.

"A medical commitment, then." His eyes narrowed. "Is that it? You're afraid that by agreeing to marry me you'll be committing yourself to this operation you've got such mixed feelings about. Am I warm?"

It took her a while to find the words to express what she felt. Everything she'd said before had been secondary. Was he warm? He was red hot!

"I just think," she began timidly, "that it would be better to wait to get married until I know what I'm going to do."

"Until you *know*? Is there any question? You're going to have that repair work done. Then you're going to live happily after. With me."

The command in his tone evoked a visceral reaction in her. She'd been alone too long to accept being told what to do. "I'm a grown woman, Rob," she warned. "I think I can make my own decisions."

"You don't sound like a grown woman. You sound more like a confused child to me."

"If that's the case, maybe you'd better reconsider. You wouldn't want to find yourself married to a confused child—"

"Oh-ho, no, you don't. You can't get out of it that way."

"I will not be instructed about what I should or shouldn't do."

He raised his eyes to the ceiling in a bid for patience. "I'm not trying to instruct you. I thought I was simply stating the obvious. Weren't you the one who said she wanted a husband and children?"

"I won't lose control of my life."

He forced himself to ease up on her. She'd been through a lot, and she had a lot to go through yet. "I'm not trying to control you," he said. He took one of her hands and threaded her fingers through his. "Maybe it sounded that way, and if so, I'm sorry. It's just that I do love you, and I want what's best for you, and I want what's best for me, too, which is to see you as much as possible. I need you, too, Heather. You may not realize it, but it's true. You've added dimension to my life. If you disappear on me, my existence will be flat."

"No. It'd go back to being as satisfying as it was."

"After I've tasted more? I doubt that'd be possible.... Let me turn the question around. If I were to walk out of this house right now, how would you feel?"

"Very worried. My neighbors would call the police. You're indecently dressed."

"Very funny. But you're avoiding the question. How would you feel if I suddenly vanished from your life?"

She didn't have to think long. The mere suggestion of his leaving created a gnawing vacuum in her stomach. "Alone. Lonely. Desolate—I don't want you to leave, Rob!"

"What do you want?"

"I want . . . I want to go on the way we have for a little while. I want to spend more time with you. I want to think about everything we've talked about and try to work it all out in my mind."

"Will you come in for an examination?"

"Maybe."

Much as it bothered him, for the time being he had to be satisfied with that. "How long will your thinking take?"

"I don't know. I can't give you a time limit."

"You're not getting any younger." He threw her own words back at her. "You want children."

"I've waited this long. A little longer won't hurt."

"And you're sure this is the way you want it . . . going along as we have?"

She lifted her chin defiantly. "You could make love to me."

"I could. It's never been a question of capability."

"You know what I mean."

"Mmm. That part could be the hardest for me—literally and figuratively."

"Don't you want to know if we're sexually compatible?"

"Spoken like a true virgin. Honey, if you'd been at all experienced you'd already know that we're sexually compatible. What do you think happened to you a little while ago? What do you think it was pressing against your thigh the whole time?"

"Your . . . thigh?"

"Close, but no cigar."

"I don't understand you, Rob. People are doing it all the time now. Sex is a vital part of any growing relationship."

"You've been brainwashed by *Cosmopolitan*. Doing something because it's fashionable is inane. In a meaningful relationship, people make love when it's right. Listen, Heather. I'm really not a prude. I've got the same drives any other man has—maybe even more so since I've met you. And I'm not holding back on principle. It's just that I won't push something like this. You're a virgin, and I adore you for that. What happened to you a little while ago was a taste of what you'll be feeling when we finally and fully make love."

She thought back to that shattering bliss, to the seconds when she was sure she'd died. "Can I stand it?"

"You can stand it."

"Medically."

"Easily."

She looked down at their intertwined fingers, tightening hers a bit as she drew on his strength. "I'm not act-ing on principle, either," she said softly. "It's not that I've simply decided I don't want to be a virgin any longer."

"I know that," he assured her gently.

"It's what I feel. It's this . . . this void inside . . . and it hurts sometimes."

"Tell me about it," he drawled.

Timidly she met his gaze. "Is it that way with you?"

"Worse."

"And you still want to wait?"

"Maybe not long." She was so desirable, so soft and appealing, looking up at him as she was, that he felt the nudge of his loins against the towel that ringed his hips. "I'm not sure how long I can hold out."

"But you won't do it today."

"No."

She put her hand lightly against his pelvis. "Could I force you to?"

"You could . . . uh, you could make me lose control, yes." His voice wasn't the only thing that was growing thicker. "But you got all riled up when you thought I was taking control from you. Would you turn around and do the same to me?"

"No." She raised her hand to his waist. "If I give you the time you want, will you give me the time *I* want?"

Rob knew when to fight and when not to, and it was a time for the latter. He had enough confidence in himself, and in Heather, to believe that one day they'd both be satisfied. "You're one tough negotiator, Heather Cole," he stated, but there was a gentle smile on his face. "Y'know, that?"

6

ROB SAW HEATHER once for dinner in the middle of the following week, then invited her down to his house on Sunday. It was everything hers wasn't—modern and sprawling—but she loved it. They spent the morning lounging in the yard, then, when the air grew hot, on the shaded deck. They grilled swordfish steaks for dinner—Heather had brought them with her, along with potato salad and marinated asparagus.

He'd tucked her in her car and was leaning in the open window, when he nonchalantly said, "I've made an appointment for you to come in on Tuesday. Can you make it?"

"An appointment?"

"For some tests."

"At the hospital?"

He drawled his words in an attempt at lightness. "That's where the equipment is."

"Uh . . . I don't know, Rob. You should have checked with me first."

"I'm checking with you now. Ten o'clock Tuesday morning. Is there a problem?"

Her hands had tightened on the steering wheel. She studied them. "I . . . I don't think so. I've got so much to do this week, though."

"You'll be back in Chester by two o'clock."

"The tests will take four hours?"

"No. But I thought we'd have some lunch afterward, and you've got to allow for driving time."

"Oh." A frown skipped across her brow. "Okay. I'll try to make it."

He grinned. "That's all I ask." Leaning farther into the car, he kissed her once, then stepped back and watched her leave.

AT NINE O'CLOCK Tuesday morning, Heather called Rob's office. She suspected that he'd be off in the hospital somewhere, and was quite satisfied to leave a message with Helen.

"Dr. McCrae was expecting me this morning, but I just got a call from my buyer, who needs half a dozen handbags yesterday. I won't be able to make it to New Haven. Could you give Rob the message?"

Helen diligently made a note on her pad. "He'll be disappointed," she said softly. "So am I. I was looking forward to meeting you."

Heather felt guiltier than ever. "And I you. Rob's spoken very highly of you."

"He's a wonderful man."

"I think so.... Well, I'm sure I'll talk with him later, but I didn't want him worrying when I don't show. You'll tell him?"

"Of course. Would you like to set up another appointment now?"

"Uh...no...no. I'll wait and see what's best for Rob."

What was best for Rob was the following morning, but, wary of pressuring her, he scheduled her in for Friday.

They saw each other Wednesday night, and though he made passing reference to the new appointment—and she nodded her agreement—neither dwelled on the matter.

She called him Thursday night to say that her neighbor's son had fallen that afternoon and broken his leg, and that she'd volunteered to baby-sit Friday while the boy's mother put in a half shift at work.

Rob set her up for the following Tuesday. When he spoke with her on Monday night, he wasn't surprised to hear that she'd gotten a call from an old college friend who was making an impromptu stop in to see her the next day.

"I think you're avoiding this, Heather."

"I can't help it, Rob. Things just seem to keep coming up."

"Isn't it a matter of priorities?"

"Exactly. I've been feeling fine. There's no rush on the tests you want to run. I apologize. Really I do. I know that your time's at stake and that you have to make arrangements to use the machines."

"I don't care about the time or the arrangements. I care about you."

"Are you worried...about something specific?" she asked, unable to hide sudden nervousness.

"Of course not. You said it yourself. You've been feeling fine. It's just that I'll feel better once we've run you through everything, once I've got a clear picture of the amount of narrowing of that valve opening, the degree of pathological change, the level of obstruction of the blood flow."

She shivered. "You sound like a doctor."

"I am a doctor, but you're making me feel totally hamstrung. I can't know anything until I've examined you, and I can't do it up there."

Hearing his frustration, she sought to alleviate it. "I'll come in, Rob," she said quietly. "I promise. Set up another time—maybe next week or the week after—and I will be there."

He let out a sigh. "Okay, Heather. I'll do it. But you'd better make it this time, or else."

"Or else what?"

"Or else . . . or else I'll refuse to see you again until you do."

She was very still for a moment. "That's blackmail."

"I only resort to it when I'm desperate."

"There's no need for desperation. I'm fine. Just fine."

FEARING HIS STRATEGY was somehow off, Rob sought out his friend Jason Parrish the next day. They settled in the doctors' lounge, which was mercifully deserted.

"I've got a problem, and I need your advice," Rob said.

"A psychiatric problem?"

"Uh . . . of sorts."

"Is it personal or professional?"

"A little of each."

Jason ran a hand across his mustache, which was as thick as his silver hair was curly. "Interesting. Shoot."

"There's a woman I know. We've been seeing each other pretty regularly and we're very close. The week before last she told me that she's had a mitral valve problem since she was nine."

"Prolapse?"

"I wish it were. No, hers is a case of stenosis. She's been doing fine, she claims, and from what I've seen being with her, I believe her. But she's been told that she should have corrective surgery before she tries to have children. So I set up an appointment for her to come in for an exam and some tests, and at the last minute she canceled. She's done the same thing twice more. She's always got an excuse. She apologizes, and I know she feels badly, but she can't help herself. She's scared."

"Of hearing something she doesn't want to hear?"

"That, I'm sure. Also of hearing that she's a prime candidate for a repair job. One part of her wants to go ahead and take care of what needs to be taken care of. The other part, the one that seems to win out in the end, is content to let the whole thing ride."

"But you're not."

"No."

"Okay, Rob. Fill in the blanks for me. What, exactly, is your stake in all this?"

Rob would have been reluctant to bare his heart to another man. With Jason it was different. They were friends—with a capital 'F.' He'd been the one to bolster Jason through a personal crisis—in that case, an ugly divorce—two years before. He deeply respected Jason's professional judgment, and on a personal level he trusted him completely.

"I'm in love with her. It's my kids I want her to have."

Jason digested that with commendable aplomb. "Ahh.... Does she want that, too?"

"She loves me, and she's said she wants children. She hasn't specified that she wants them to be mine because this business about her heart condition came out, and I think she feels that I'll pressure her all the more. I don't know what to do, Jason. It's not that I'm worried about her immediate condition. I've seen her in action, and the symptoms aren't that debilitating. But I have this compulsion to know everything about her, medically speaking."

"That's understandable, given your specialty."

"I've tried to be gentle with her. I've tried not to make an issue of it. The last thing I want is for her to feel forced into something, or worse, to feel that there's cause for alarm. When she's canceled appointments I've taken it without a fuss." He hesitated, lips thinning. "Well, almost. Last time she backed out I told her that if she did it again I wouldn't see her." He gave his friend a look of chagrin. "It was a bad move, wasn't it?"

Jason nodded.

"So what do I do now?"

"How old is she?"

"Twenty-nine."

"Emotionally stable?"

"Very."

"Ever been married before?"

"No. Ours is the first serious relationship she's had. She's led an insulated life."

"Any other physical problems?"

"Not that I know of. She takes good care of herself. She's slim. She eats just what she should and avoids what she shouldn't. She goes out walking every day. She follows doctor's orders to the letter."

"Until now."

"Right."

"Does she follow doctor's orders in the hope that the condition will go away?"

"I don't think that's it. She's honest with herself, at least when it comes to accepting her problem and living with it."

"Then she follows doctor's orders in the hope that the condition won't worsen."

"I assume that's what it is."

"But she does know that the problem can be corrected, that it should be corrected if she wants to have children."

"Uh-huh."

Jason raised both brows and blew out a breath. "What you've got on your hands could be a case of simple fear. You've seen it in others, and you'll see it in many more. What makes this one different is your personal involvement." He thought about that while he turned the coffee-filled plastic cup in his hands. "In the past, she's counted on your forgiving her when she's broken appointments. She's played on the strength of your love." He raised his gaze to Rob. "Is she reliable in other things?"

"Totally. She's never been late, or canceled out of anything else."

"Okay. But she feels she can get away with this. Maybe it'd be better if you made an appointment for her with another man. She'd feel more of a commitment that way."

"Possibly. But I really want to do the tests myself. I'm not sure I'd trust anyone else to do them."

"You trust Howard. He could see her."

Rob looked dubious. "I don't know . . ."

"Look, if she has the surgery, you'll have to trust someone else. Even if you were a surgeon, you wouldn't be the one to operate. You're too emotionally involved to wield a knife on her."

Rob flinched. The thought of anyone cutting into Heather bothered him.

"For that matter," Jason continued, watching Rob closely, "you may be too emotionally involved even to do the workup."

"That's baloney. I can do it. We're not talking critical moves here, my friend. And besides, Heather trusts me. She might be even more reluctant to go to a stranger. Sure, I know she'll have to when it's time for the operation, but at least I can introduce her to John McHale and she can get to know him first." He nodded. "Mmm. John would be the one to do it."

"You're jumping the gun. Let's get her in for the tests first." He sipped his coffee. "Do you think it's possible that she's embarrassed to have you do the exam?"

"No. She knows that I don't think less of her or feel less for her because she's got a heart problem."

"Physically, Rob. Could your examining her be a potential physical embarrassment?"

Rob grinned. "Nah. She's pretty comfortable with me that way."

"Lucky you," Jason said. Then his wily smile faded and he grew pensive, thinking his thoughts aloud. "Okay, chalk modesty. She's scared of the exam itself and what might come after. One possibility would be to have her talk with someone you've treated, someone who's had the same problem and had it corrected . . . but she's apt to balk at that. Later it might be something to consider.

But now...I take it she's alone. No family who could help you? Or friends?"

"Her parents are dead, and as far as I know there's no other family. At least none that she's close to. She has friends, but she's pretty much hidden the problem from them."

"Is there some reason, beyond the immediate, why she'd be frightened of the hospital? Were either of her parents sick and hospitalized before they died?"

"Her father had a heart attack and died instantly. He was at work. He never made it to the hospital."

"What about her mother?"

"Cancer. Pretty quick, too, from what I gather. If anything, though, Heather felt that if her mother had paid enough attention to her symptoms, she would have sought medical help sooner and might have made it. She does respect modern medicine."

"Could there be guilt? If the mother devoted herself to taking care of her daughter to the extent that she over-looked her own health, Heather may feel guilty."

"Possibly. But what would that have to do with this?"

Jason was really getting into it. "She may feel that she doesn't deserve to have that operation, that she doesn't deserve to be put to right. Or it may simply be a case of her doing what her mother did, of minimizing the problem indefinitely."

Rob was clearly skeptical. "I don't think that's it. I really don't. Heather has never been particularly hung up when she's talked about her mother—or her father, for that matter. I don't think it has anything to do with the past. Hell, there's enough reason for her to be frightened right now. Control seems to be a big thing with her. She believes that once her condition is conclusively measured, she'll be steamrollered into the operating room. Open-heart surgery isn't something you look forward to."

"But a normal life afterward is. Giving birth to children is. Maybe that's what you've got to concentrate on. The future." Rob nodded, but Jason wasn't done. "How did she take it when you gave her that ultimatum?"

"She accused me of blackmail. I think it scared her."

"That you'd resort to blackmail?"

"And that we wouldn't see each other."

"She does love you."

"I don't have any doubt about it."

"Then that's what you've got to focus on. Reason with her. If she's an intelligent woman—and I doubt you'd fall for one who wasn't—she'll have to respond to logic. The fact that you love her and want her happy and healthy is the most logical argument you can make." He took another drink of coffee while he pondered the dilemma for several moments longer. "If it were me, I'd put the ball in her hands."

"She'll hold on to it without moving!"

"Not if you coach her on the side. If you give her enough encouragement, she'll make a move. If she's been directing her own life for the past few years, and if she's legitimately worried about being steamrollered, she's more apt to respond positively if she feels she's retaining some control over things. Give her all the arguments about why you want her to come in, but let *her* tell *you* when that time will be."

"And if I do that and she still does nothing?"

"You could throw out the possibility of her seeing another doctor. Or talking with another patient, or a former patient. Or meeting with me."

"That'd really scare her," Rob quipped, only half in jest.

"I could talk through her fears with her. I could find out if there is something else, something deeper, something from the past that is affecting her judgment."

"You don't know Heather. She's a clear thinker. She's got her act together."

"Obviously not, if she refuses to face up to what she should be doing."

"There are two sides to that, though. In a way she's right. There's no medical emergency saying she should have surgery this month or next. It's me who wants it over and done with.... I think she'd be livid if I suggested she see you."

Jason's mustache twitched. "Maybe that'd be enough of a threat to get her in for those tests on her own."

"Maybe I should just kidnap her and bring her in bound and gagged."

Jason set his empty cup on the nearby table, stood and stretched. "If you decide to do that, pal, you'd better pray that her love's strong enough, really strong enough to forgive. You can lead a horse to the water, but you can't make him drink."

"If you push his head under, he won't have any choice. And if he finds that the dunking quenches his thirst, he'll be grateful."

"And what wise man said that?"

"Me," Rob answered with a rueful smile.

HE GAVE MUCH THOUGHT to what Jason had said. As subtly as he could, he asked Heather questions about her mother's illness and Heather's feelings about it, but nothing emerged to suggest that she felt guilt. Moreover, it was as though Heather had been a fly on the wall in the doctors' lounge that day.

"I know why you're asking me these things," she accused, but very gently, indulgently. "You're wondering if I'm hung up about something to do with my mother. I'm not. I don't identify with her. Her situation was very different from mine. Sure, I wish she'd seen a doctor sooner, but because the nature of her problem demanded it. Mine doesn't. I've seen my share of doctors. I know what I have and where I stand. It's a different ball game."

"What was it like when you first found out about your heart?"

"Scary."

"Were you hospitalized?"

"For a few days. It seemed that someone was either putting me through another test or sticking another needle into me. I hated it. And you can take that smug look off your face, Robert McCrae, because I've grown up a lot since then. I won't like your tests any better now, but when it's time to do them, I'll do them."

"I'm not making another appointment for you."

"Oh?"

"*You* can make the appointment. You can call Helen when you're ready and she'll set things up."

Heather eyed him with slight trepidation. He'd been so anxious to get her in. She wondered if his feelings for her were changing. "Why the switch?"

"You're a grown woman. You said it yourself. You also said you wanted to be in control. Okay, control."

"You want me to prove to you that I'm mature enough to take the bull by the horns, which means that if I put off coming in for the tests, I'll have failed your test. So I'm damned if I do and damned if I don't."

"You're not damned if you do. You'll have a series of tests. Then, if you decide to go ahead, you'll have the operation. Once it's behind you, you'll be able to look to the future without worry. That's what *I* want." He put his hands on her neck and stroked it with his thumbs. "I want pleasure and happiness with you. Sure, there will be minor roadblocks. We'll have differences of opinion from time to time. We'll have sources of concern about our kids—no parents escape them. But the situation with your heart is something that can be remedied. It just doesn't make sense to let it go on and on, hanging over our heads when it doesn't have to!" Helplessness and frustration were quick to rise. Tempering them with effort, he gentled his voice. "I love you, Heather. I want only the best for you. You have to believe that."

He wasn't sure if she did, but he focused on that theme in the days to come. Once, subtly, he suggested that she might want to see Howard instead of him. She politely shook her head. He suggested that she talk with one of his former patients, a woman who had been successfully treated for the same problem, and he even went so far as to press a piece of paper with the woman's name and number into Heather's hand. She stuffed it in her pocket—he presumed to be discarded later. He didn't quite have the courage to suggest she talk with Jason.

The frustration and helplessness grew. She had the ball. He was coaching her. And getting nowhere.

One week passed, then another, and Heather made no attempt to call Helen for an appointment.

Time and again Rob ran through his conversation with Jason, but each time he seemed to come back to its bantering finale. What he'd originally said in jest seemed, as the weeks passed, to have more and more merit. Oh, he couldn't bind, gag and kidnap Heather. But perhaps he could modify the scenario.

He was deeply convinced that once she had the tests she'd be relieved. True, he'd told her she held the reins, and she might be angry at first that he'd taken them from her, but he felt reasonably assured that, what with the love they shared, he'd be able to work through that with her.

In the end it was simply a matter of priorities. Rob knew that if he had to choose between Heather's feelings for him and her health, he'd opt for the latter. He loved her that much.

And he prayed it wouldn't come down to the choice.

"HI, HONEY."

Heather gripped the phone tightly. "Rob! Is everything okay? It's eleven-thirty in the morning. Aren't you supposed to be at a meeting?"

"I just got done. It was a tough one."

"You sound down."

"I am. I need you to pick me up."

"Can you come out tonight?" He hadn't planned to, she knew, but she'd love to see him.

"I don't think I'll make it until tonight. How 'bout if you come down now. We could go out for lunch—you haven't eaten yet, have you?" He'd timed the call, knowing that she usually had lunch at noon.

"No, I haven't eaten. Are you sure you can take the time?"

"Oh, I'm sure. If I don't get some kind of break, I'll be useless all afternoon. I really need to see you, honey. Can you come?"

She felt no hesitance. She loved Rob, and he needed her. She glanced at the clock. "I'll have to change, but I can be there in an hour."

He sighed in relief. "That'll be great. There's a little Greek restaurant not far from here. Sound okay?"

"Sounds fine. I'll see you soon."

"Thanks, honey.... And drive carefully."

The restaurant was perfect for Rob's needs. It was small, slightly noisy and more than slightly crowded. It didn't afford a great deal of privacy, but he hadn't wanted that. He was feeling like a heel, having some second thoughts about his plan. The less he brooded on it the better.

When Heather asked about the meeting that had been so difficult, he was able to say with only minor exaggeration that he was waging an argument for a new and expensive piece of equipment and that he was running into flak from the hospital directors. She seemed sympathetic and was understanding of his less than cheery disposition.

When they'd finished and left the restaurant, Rob took a deep breath. "That's better."

"So now you can get back to work. Me, too."

"Do you have to rush home?"

She hesitated. "No . . . my work can wait. Your schedule is the one that's more pressing."

"I've got an idea. Since you're here and I don't want to let you go just yet, why don't you come up for a minute and meet Helen? She's been asking when she'd see you."

"Oh . . . I don't know, Rob." She was hesitant to step foot inside the hospital. "You'll be late for your afternoon appointments."

But he'd already taken her arm and was guiding her across the street. "I've got time" was all he said.

Once inside the hospital, they wound through one corridor into the next, up a staircase, down another hall. Heather's sense of direction had deserted her by the time they reached Rob's office.

She met Helen, whom she found to be perfectly charming, and saw the place where Rob worked—his desk, shelves packed with medical books and journals, walls covered with formally scripted degrees and citations, his two large file cabinets, several side chairs and a couch.

When he led her back down the hall, she put her trust in him to guide her through the labyrinth of the front door. They didn't end up at the front door, though, but on yet another floor of the hospital. Rob was being particularly quiet, and he held her hand tightly. She began to grow wary.

"Rob?"

He was leading her through a door into a small examining room. A nurse was waiting there, a plain-looking woman several years older than Heather. She'd been seated in a chair but quickly stood when Rob entered with Heather in tow.

"Why are we here?" Heather asked in a whisper. But she knew. She knew. She dug in her heels and tugged to free her arm, but Rob wasn't letting go. "You tricked me," she said between gritted teeth. "You planned this all along."

Rob cast a short glance at the nurse, then spoke quietly to Heather. He couldn't turn back now, and that fact imbued him with utter calm. "I didn't plan a trying morning or a Greek salad, but I did have to get you in here somehow."

"I'd like to go home now," she said, still in a whisper, still with her teeth gritted, but now with every other muscle tense, as well.

Rob firmly drew her forward until she stood within inches of the examining table. He darted a second glance at the waiting nurse, then looked back at Heather. "This is Andrea Williams. She'll stay with you while you undress. I'm going outside to check on something, but I'll be back in a minute."

Heather opened her mouth to protest, but he'd released her hand and was disappearing through the door before she could find the proper words. The door swung shut. She stared at it.

"Coward," she muttered under her breath, tightening her fists around the strap of her bag, realizing that she was beginning to tremble but unable to stop it. When she looked over at Andrea, she knew she was trapped. To turn and run would be cowardly as well as childish. Grasping at what dignity she had left, she tipped up her chin, dropped her bag on the floor and very slowly reached for the buttons of her blouse.

By the time Rob returned, she was sitting on the table with her legs hanging down one side, wearing a paper robe with its opening in front. She was so angry that her breathing was shallow.

Rob carried a clipboard. He drew up a chair, sat down, pulled a pen from the breast pocket of the white jacket he'd changed into. Heather glared at the jacket, then at him. He looked at her for a minute before calmly beginning to ask her questions, one after the other, about her medical history. Though he knew the general facts and some of the details, there were other things he needed to know to form the basis of a complete picture of her condition.

Heather was shaking all over—fury, she told herself—and her extremities were freezing. She answered him primarily in monosyllables, her face ashen, a rigid mask of indignance. Though her voice was strained and foreign sounding, she forced herself to respond to even those questions of a strictly female nature. She was determined to show Rob up, to let him know that he couldn't cower her. She had her pride. At the moment, that was about all.

At last he put down the clipboard and stood, drawing a stethoscope from the side pocket of his jacket, putting it around his neck, coming to stand directly before her. She clenched her teeth and stared at the far wall while he examined her.

Step by step and in a soft voice, he explained what he was doing, what he was looking for, what he found. In other circumstances he wouldn't have spoken as much,

but, understanding Heather, he felt it would help if she
was totally involved. He knew she was furious, and upset, and he did what he could to be as soothing as possible. Between quiet instructions and explanations, he
murmured soft words of encouragement, urging her to
relax—in vain.

He took her blood pressure, measured her pulse rate,
felt for the key pulses in the neck and groin. Parting her
gown, he placed his hand on her chest to feel the im-
pulses transmitted through its wall. He watched the motion of her chest cage through several breaths. He
thumped front and back to determine if there was con-
gestion in her lungs. He listened to her heart with his
stethoscope, assessing the sounds of the diseased valve.
He had her lie on her side, then her back so that he could
hear certain sounds better. He pressed his hands on her
abdomen, locating her liver, noting its size and condition. He checked her ankles and feet for abnormal
warmth and swelling.

Through all the touching, tapping and probing he was
gentle. Heather, on the other hand, held herself like a
stone. The trembling had eased, though she was breathing more rapidly than normal. She endured what he was
doing with her jaw set tight.

At one point when he lifted her hand to check her cir-
culation by pressing her fingernails, he had to determinedly unclench her fingers. Four small crescent-shaped
marks marred the pale pink of her palm. He rubbed the
spot, gave her a look she might have seen to be apologetic had she been functioning properly, and resumed his
exam.

At long last he had her sit up. When she swayed for a minute, he steadied her.

"Okay?" he asked softly.

She gave a single, fierce nod.

"Everything looks fine, Heather. The stenosis is there, but it doesn't sound terribly advanced and it doesn't seem to have seriously affected any of your other organs. I want you to get dressed now. We'll take a walk downstairs for chest X rays, an electrocardiogram and echocardiography. We can have a blood workup done there, too."

She stared steadily at him, but she didn't say a word. Rob got her meaning, though. With a nod at Andrea, he left so that Heather could put her clothes on.

It was late afternoon before all the tests had been done to Rob's satisfaction. Heather was thoroughly exhausted, but the exhaustion did little to blunt her anger. She walked stiffly by his side, putting up with his hand on her arm only because she refused to make a scene. They returned to his office. Helen watched as they silently passed her desk.

"Do you want to lie down for a while before we leave?" Rob asked when his door was shut behind them.

Heather's nostrils flared with the tight breath she took. "We? I have my own car here. With your permission, I'll leave now."

"You haven't got my permission. You're tired and you're angry. And if you don't let off some of that steam, you'll pop a blood vessel."

She stood her ground and simply stared at him. It was the same stare he'd been receiving from her all afternoon, as if one part of her were totally tuned out, in another world, while the other part wanted to strangle him.

"Sit down, Heather," he said, trying his best to be patient.

Leaving her bag on her shoulder, she sat in one of the side chairs and pressed her hands to her lap. He perched on the corner of his desk nearest her.

"How do you feel?"

"Fine."

"Does anything hurt?"

"No."

"Do you have questions about any of the tests?"

"No."

"Do you still love me?"

She said nothing.

He had to settle for that. It was better than a flat-out no. "What would you like to do now?"

"Go home."

He pushed himself from the desk and was in the process of exchanging the white coat for his blazer, when she added, "Alone."

"I'm afraid I can't let you do that. I'll drive you."

"I won't leave my car here."

"We'll take your car, then."

"And how will you get back?"

"You can drive me back in the morning."

For the first time she showed a sign of life. Her eyes flashed dangerously. "You are not spending the night at my house."

"I'll spend as long as I have to. We're going to have this out, Heather. I don't care how long it takes."

"You're a busy man," she reminded him snidely. "I've already taken enough of your time."

"You're the woman I love. You could never take too much of it."

"And all the other things you have to do?"

He straightened the collar of his blazer. "They'll ride.... Come on. Let's get out of here."

When he reached for her arm, Heather stood. She went with him through the labyrinth to the door she'd thought she'd been headed for hours before. She let herself be placed in the passenger's seat of her car, let Rob take the keys, start the ignition and head for the expressway. She let the silence act as a buffer through what seemed an interminable drive home.

By the time they arrived, she'd just about reached the limit of her self-control.

7

"YOU TAKE MY CAR and go home," Heather said as she rushed to the front door and fumbled with the lock. "I can pick it up later in the week."

Rob was no more than two paces behind her. "I'm coming in."

She managed to get the door open and turned to insist that he leave, but he was literally shoving her through the door and following her inside.

"Rob, I've really had enough for one day—"

"Not quite. Not yet."

She stood in the front hall with her head bowed, her fingers massaging a throbbing spot on her forehead. "If you don't leave now, I'll get angry."

"You already are angry." He strode into the living room and sank onto the sofa, sitting back, crossing one leg over the other. There was nothing leisurely about his pose. It spoke of determination, just as his expression broadcast stubbornness.

She glared sideways at him. "Please leave," she said quietly, but her voice was shaking under the restraint she was imposing on herself.

"No."

The bounds of her restraint began to fray. "I don't want you here!"

"I'm sorry."

Her restraint crumbled. She stalked into the living room and stood before him with her hands propped on her hips. "You are not! You're feeling perfectly smug. You got your way. You can be very proud of yourself."

"I'm not."

Her eyes narrowed. "No? Well, to be honest, I don't believe you. I'm not sure I can believe anything you say anymore." She took a deep breath and exhaled pure rage. "I trusted you, Rob! I truly trusted you! From the very first, I felt safe with you, but it was all an illusion, wasn't it? What was it you said?" She lowered her voice in mocking imitation of his. "'*You* make the appointment. You're a grown woman. You want to control. So, control.'" Her chest heaved as her breathing quickened. "That was a whole lot of control you gave me today! I didn't ever really have a say in the matter—I take that back. I did have a say at one point. When you called me to say that you were down and needed me. I had a say then. I could have told you that I was busy and couldn't drive into the city to meet you. But I didn't. And do you want to know why? Because I said to myself, 'He needs me and I love him—of course I'll go.'" She gave a harsh laugh. "I was a sucker. I bought your whole song and dance, fell for it hook, line and sinker. I believed you— I actually believed you!"

Again she dropped her voice in mockery. "'Come up for a minute and meet Helen.'" She resumed a higher pitch. "Helen knew all along what was going on, didn't she? Do you have any idea how foolish I feel? The ignorant one. Everybody knows what's going on but her—" she pounded her chest "—*me!*"

Rob made no move to defend himself, but she hadn't expected him to and she didn't intend to wait. There were too many thoughts, too many words threatening to choke her if they weren't spit out. She pushed careless waves of dark hair back from her face and eyed him accusingly. "You planned the whole thing in advance. The nurse was ready and waiting. So were the technicians at each of the machines, and that little lady who insisted on drawing half the blood from my body."

Her hands fell to fists by her sides and she gasped for air. "I've never been so humiliated in my entire life! And so disappointed! You tricked me, manipulated me, after I had such faith in you!"

The exertion of her outburst was taking its toll. Her energy was fading. Her voice lost some of its force, but it was coated with sarcasm. "The busy doctor. Always in demand. Running from conference to conference, patient to patient. But you managed to clear the entire afternoon, didn't you? You didn't have to personally lead me by the arm through each and every one of those tests, y'know. The technicians could have managed without your hovering over their shoulders. Your little Andrea could have corraled me from one place to the next. And why was she there during your examination, anyway? To protect my virtue?" She threw back her head. "That's a laugh. All the talk of doctors taking advantage of female patients. I'd have to be the one to rape you if I wanted anything!"

She whirled to storm to the window but found her legs unsteady, so she stopped behind the chair and gripped its back for support. "Maybe my first instinct was right. That very first day I saw you at the hospital. I didn't say anything then about my condition. I should never have said anything about it!" She knew that would have been unrealistic, if not impossible, but somehow it sounded right at that instant.

Rob sat quietly. He said nothing. His insides were a mass of hard knots, but he braved her withering stare as though doing penance. Only the lines of strain on his face betrayed what he was feeling.

Heather suddenly wasn't satisfied with his silence. Or maybe it was that she'd exhausted her own supply of fire. Her anger had dissipated, leaving in its place a mélange of other, deeper emotions, of which hurt was foremost.

"Well," she prodded brokenly, "haven't you got anything to say?"

He looked at her for a long time. The red flags of anger that had waved on her cheeks through the first of her tirade had faded. Her face was pale, her shoulders slumped. She looked tired and fragile, and he wondered if he'd pushed too far insisting he come home with her. It amazed him that she was still on her feet.

He dropped his gaze to his loafer, absently ran a finger along the seam between leather and sole. He extended his lower lip to cover his upper one, slowly let it slide back to its natural position. Then he looked up at her.

"You're right," he said somberly. "What I did was underhanded. I made arrangements for the tests beforehand. Then I manipulated you into taking them. I didn't lie about the meeting this morning. It was rough, and I did need you—"

"Hah!"

"It's true," he continued in the same low tone. "I've come to need you that way. It relieves me to talk over things that are bothering me."

"Not this time, obviously. You didn't talk. You simply took things into your own hands."

He might have said that he had tried to reason with her, that he'd made appointments—which she'd canceled, that he'd given her all the encouragement he possibly could have, and that he'd finally done the only thing left to do. But he didn't say any of that. Though there was no victory in it, he had gotten what he'd wanted.

"The need in me this time was that you let me examine you and have those tests. Maybe it was an irrational one, but I couldn't help myself." He uncrossed his legs and sat forward, elbows on his thighs, hands dangling helplessly between his knees. "I was wrong. You have every right to be furious. The best defense, the only defense I can give is that I love you. I knew you were scared, and I was concerned. I felt that the best thing for both of us was to get it over with." His gaze held hers and grew plaintive. "I do love you, Heather," he vowed, voice cracking. "If you look deep, deep down in your own heart, you'll know it's true."

Heather covered her face with her hands. She was weakening, but she didn't want to, not when one part of her felt the lingering sting of betrayal.

Then Rob was before her, drawing her against him. She held her body stiff. "I love you. I love you, Heather." He forced her head to his chest and stroked her hair. "Was it really that bad? Don't you feel a little relieved to have it behind you?"

"But what's ahead?" she asked without answering directly. "Are you going to trick me into the operation now? Will you drug me one night and truck me off to the hospital? Will I wake up one morning with the whole thing done?"

He took a long, unsteady breath. "No. No, Heather. I won't do that."

"How can I be sure?"

"Because today has put enough strain on our relationship. I don't want it there, and I won't knowingly invite it again. No, from here on in, it's up to you. The final decision's yours. It'd be unethical of me to have it any other way."

"You weren't worried about ethics today," was her muffled retort.

"A series of tests are very different from surgery. And you were wide-awake through the whole thing. If you'd absolutely refused today, I wouldn't have forced you."

She hadn't "absolutely refused." They both knew it. Rob wanted to think that to some degree she had been relieved to have had the decision taken from her. Heather wasn't quite ready to be that introspective, or that honest.

"Anyway," he went on without forcing an admission from her, "we'll take it one step at a time. I want to see your records, but I'll need your permission. I'd like to compare the new data with the old and find out exactly what kind of change has taken place over the past twenty years." She wasn't arguing, which was good, he mused gratefully. "I'll tell you precisely where you stand. I can introduce you to John McHale—he's our best cardiothoracic surgeon. You can talk with him—if you want—and he'll explain the details of the operation. You'll be the sole one to decide if and when to go ahead."

"That was pretty much what you said last time."

He pressed his lips to the top of her head. Some of the rigidity had left her body, and she was leaning against him wearily. He wrapped his arms more snugly around her. "This time I'll stick to it. You may have thought I was enjoying myself today, but I wasn't. Believe me, I wasn't. The whole time I was examining you, trying to concentrate on what I was feeling and seeing and hearing, I had to fight off your anger and your stares. It was probably the hardest exam I've ever conducted. It's taken a toll on me, too." He closed his eyes. "No, I won't go through that again. Not again."

"I'm not sure I believe you."

"How can you not? Can't you feel my pain?"

"My own is too raw to feel much of anything else," she countered. "I trusted you, *trusted* you."

"I've never betrayed your love. You have to understand that I did what I did *because* of that love."

She would have raised her head to look at him had she had the strength. But she felt limp. If Rob's body, his arms hadn't been supporting her she would have long since collapsed into the chair. "Then the nature of that love frightens me. I'm not sure about it anymore. How deep can it be if you can't respect me as a human being?"

"I respect you in every way. I respected your fear. I did what I thought best to overcome it."

"What if I hold out against the operation? There's no rush. You said it yourself—the stenosis doesn't seem that bad and nothing else has been seriously affected. What if I decide to wait? After all, it's not as if there's a risk of my getting pregnant."

At her last words and their subtle taunt, Rob forced her face up. She was pale and fragile-looking, yes, but she was every bit as beautiful to him as she'd ever been. Her eyes never left his.

"If I decide to wait," she asked cautiously, "will you do what you think best then, too?"

"What I think best from here on is for us to be totally honest with each other. I'll give you my reasons for feeling one way or another about the operation, and I want you to give me yours. Honest feelings, Heather, even if they're irrational. My compulsion that you have the tests was probably just as crazy as your fear of them. Maybe if we'd been more honest, we'd have been able to reach a compromise."

"Sometimes compromises aren't possible. I either have the operation or I don't. There doesn't seem to be much middle ground."

"There is when it comes to timing. I won't rush you. You'll be calling the shots."

She studied his face, searching for evidence of falsity. What she saw, though, was a jaw that was firm and straight, lips that rested together as though they'd spoken God's truth and had no more to add, and silver eyes that held a hint of vulnerability.

She didn't know why—perhaps it was that openness—but she believed him. She'd trusted him once and he'd abused that trust. Yet it lived on. Maybe she was a fool, she mused. Maybe being in love made her a fool. Maybe being in love made him a fool, and therefore explained what he'd done earlier that day.

She felt confused, and overwhelmingly tired. Closing her eyes for a minute, she took a deep breath. When she looked back at him, his face was filled with concern.

"I think I'd like to lie down now," she whispered. She needed time to think. And to rest. Mustering what little strength she could find in reserve, she stepped away from him. "I'm very tired."

She sounded tired. She looked it. Rob didn't try to hold her, or to help her to bed. Instead he watched her make her way slowly to the foot of the stairs, grasp the banister and start up. He respected her need for independence and self-sufficiency. He respected her need to be alone.

He stood looking toward the second floor landing long after she'd disappeared from sight. Then he turned slowly, shrugged out of his blazer and dropped it on the chair as he made his way to the window. Hands buried in the pockets of his slacks, he stared out at the yard. The trees were lush and mature, as August made them. The shrubs were full and healthy, the lawn thick, with only the occasional dandelion cluster to break its verdant expanse.

Everything outside was peaceful, restful, representing so much of what Heather and her home had come to mean to him in the past weeks. Yet peace and restfulness were the last things he felt just then. Doubts assailed him, followed closely by regret.

He wondered if he'd blown it all.

Discouraged, he returned to the sofa and sprawled across it, one arm flung over his eyes. Everything upstairs was quiet. Everything downstairs was quiet. He listened to the steady beat of his own heart and cursed its ailment. Oh, yes, he had a heart condition, too. Heather.

One hour passed, and he remained where he was. He thought; he brooded; he agonized over the afternoon that had been. A second hour passed with still no sound of life from upstairs. He shifted position, then pushed himself from the sofa and went to the window again. This time the yard was bathed in the purple light of dusk. He glanced at his watch, then, worriedly, down the hall toward the stairs. Before long he was headed in that direction.

He walked softly. If Heather was sleeping, he didn't want to disturb her. But he had to make sure she was all right.

The door to her bedroom was closed. He turned the knob very slowly and carefully pushed the door open. The room was dim, but he clearly made out Heather's form on the big brass bed. She was curled on her side and wore a T-shirt that reached her thighs. The clothes she'd worn that day were scattered on the floor where she'd dropped them in her exhaustion.

Treading quietly, he approached the bed. One of her arms was draped around her waist; the other lay on the sheet beside her. Her legs were tucked up, but the position couldn't hide their smooth length or slender shape. He stared at them, looking away only when his loins tightened involuntarily. The sight of her face, though, brought another tightening, this one around his chest.

Her eyes were closed, dark lashes spiky against her skin. Her cheeks had regained some of their color, but it only seemed to emphasize the dried tracks where tears had gone. She'd cried herself to sleep.

"Oh, baby," he whispered, feeling such pain, such love that he didn't know what to do. . . . Yes, he did. He did know what to do. He could indeed show her how much he loved her.

Stepping quietly out of his shoes, he tugged his shirt from his slacks and began to unbutton it. He kept his eyes on her face, watchful of the moment she might awaken, but she remained in a deep sleep. Under other circumstances he'd have let her sleep. God only knew that she needed, deserved, the rest. She'd had a bitch of a day, and she'd been upset even when she'd left him to climb the stairs.

He'd always been the one to say that there'd be a right time for their first lovemaking, but he'd never imagined it would be a time like this. He couldn't deny his urgency, though, because it went far beyond the physical. He wanted to believe that she'd sleep even better in his arms—after he'd shown her what it was to be his love.

Tossing the shirt to a nearby chair, he unbuckled his belt, then released the fastening of his slacks and lowered the zipper.

She didn't move.

He eased himself down on the edge of the bed and, one after another, peeled off his socks and sent them in the direction of his shirt. Then he put one arm behind her, one in front of her, and he leaned down to gently kiss her ear. She twitched her head in her sleep and he smiled. He drew his fingers through her hair, pushing it from her face, replacing it with a kiss on her temple, then her cheek, then her eye.

Her lids fluttered, then settled again.

Again he smiled. For all the times she'd practically begged him to make love to her, it seemed she was determined to sleep through his surrender. Surrender? Not quite. His body was growing bold on him, thanks to the sweet smell of her and the beckoning warmth of her skin. He kissed her again, and again, teasing her chin, her jaw, the corner of her mouth.

She gave a half smile in her sleep, and her lids fluttered again. This time they opened, but with great effort. She took in a faintly hiccuping breath and forced her eyes wider. "Rob?" she whispered.

"It's me," he answered as softly.

She closed her eyes and for a minute he feared she was falling back to sleep, but in another instant her lids flew open. She stared at him, confused, then dropped her gaze from his face to his bare chest to the open fly of his slacks. When her eyes rose again, confusion was mixed with something else—he wasn't sure whether it was desire or fear, and he refused to think that it might be anger or worse, refusal. She whispered his name again, questioningly, and he gathered her into his arms.

"I love you, Heather. I want to show you how much."

"But . . . I don't understand. . . ." Whatever unsureness plagued her didn't keep her from slowly winding her arms around his waist.

"I'm going to make love to you, honey. I know you're tired, and it's been one hell of a day for you, but I want to turn all that around. You're strong. You can take it . . . if you want to."

She held her breath for a minute, and he waited in agony. When her answer finally came it was a wordless one, the release of a deep, pleasure-filled sigh, open-mouthed against his chest.

Rob shuddered in relief. He held her until he felt in control, then angled himself back, bent his head and kissed her. If he'd been worried that she'd be groggy, he'd worried needlessly. She returned his kiss with the same force, the same hunger, the same love that he offered. The silent communication of their lips expressed apology and forgiveness far better than words would have done. The restless roaming of their hands on each other's bodies articulately expressed their desire and need.

Rob touched her all over, reacquainting himself with her breasts and her belly and her thighs. He'd eased her to her back and was on his side on the bed, feeling himself growing hotter with each caress he received but, more important, feeling her growing hotter with each caress he gave. He was determined to arouse her slowly, but when her response grew quickly fevered, he simply determined to arouse her fully.

Using his hands and his mouth, he did just that. He suckled her breasts through the cotton of her T-shirt, leaving moist spots dotted by her hard nipples. She grew moist in other places, places his stroking made all the more so. There was even more he wanted to do, but he feared for both his sanity and his control.

"Let's take this off," he murmured thickly, tugging at the hem of her shirt, which had already ridden to her hips. She raised her buttocks, then lifted her arms and let him toss the T-shirt aside. She was wearing small bikini panties, which soon followed the shirt.

Settling full length over her, he anchored her hands by her shoulders and kissed her again, more deeply this time, thrusting his tongue far into her mouth, sliding it out, thrusting again. Tiny mewling sounds came from her throat seconds before he released her.

"I want you," she cried in a frantic breath, and began to push at the waistband of his slacks. "Please, Rob . . . please . . . now . . . hurry!"

He slid to his side only long enough to shove his slacks down, doubling up to get them off his legs, then doing the same with his briefs. By the time he was over her once again, his thighs pressing hers farther apart, she was panting softly.

He took the weight of his upper body on his elbows and gently stroked the dampness from her brow. "Relax, honey. Try to relax. Do you want me inside?"

"Oh, yes . . . now . . ."

"Are you frightened?"

"A little . . . but there's such emptiness there . . . I need you . . . to fill it. . . ."

He raised his hips and positioned himself, probing gently at the heart of her womanhood. Twining his fingers in hers, he asked, "Do you love me, Heather?"

"Always!"

"And I love you. So . . . very . . . much. . . ."

Slowly he began to penetrate her. She was slick and ready, but tight. Arousal could only partly soothe the way the first time. "Kiss me," he ordered. Anticipation of her pain made his voice gruff. The last thing he wanted was to give her any discomfort, but it was a necessary evil to pave the way for paradise.

She kissed him, pouring all her fears, her trust into it.

He eased deeper, then said into her mouth, "Just a little pain. Just for a minute," and he thrust forcefully past the final barrier of her innocence.

She tensed and cried out, but the sound was lost in his mouth. He held himself still, stroking her lips with his own, gentling her while her body adjusted to his presence. After a time, he withdrew very slowly, then eased forward again. She found the pain to be duller this time and increasingly so as he slid cautiously in and out. He was caressing her breast with the same slow movement, brushing over her nipple with his thumb, helping her to the peak she'd been at before he'd broken her maidenhood.

"Mmm...." She sighed.

"Better?"

"Yes...it feels...nice...."

"Just wait," he said with a smile, and he gradually increased both the speed and depth of his thrusts until, past the fear of hurting her, he filled her fully and completely. "Bend your knees up," he whispered hoarsely. He felt so good inside her that it was all he could do to think clearly. "That's it...prop your feet behind my knees...ahhhh...so warm...perfect...."

Within minutes he was locked into the rhythm of passion. His pleasure grew with the first movement of her hips and he murmured husky words of encouragement, which increased her response, which increased *his* response, and the spiral widened.

There was no stopping them then. Rob had thought the chances slim that Heather would reach a climax that first time, but she was breathing more quickly and arching into his powerful thrusts in a way that belied her novitiate state. He kissed her and continued to touch her, and rode higher and higher with her until he felt her stiffen and convulse and cry out his name and that she loved him.

He was in heaven. She loved him. Head thrown back, teeth gritted against the painful extreme of pleasure, he surged into her a final time, then held himself still while mind-blowing spasms shook his large body.

Panting, then moaning, then grinning, then laughing breathlessly, he undulated his hips against her in a greedy attempt to savor each and every last pulsation. He would have stayed inside her forever had not his body betrayed him by going slowly but surely limp. With a groan of regret and pleasure and love, he slid to her side and brought her over to face him. They lay that way, gazing silently, happily into each other's eyes until at last, and inevitably, they fell asleep.

Shortly before dawn the next morning they were in much the same position. When Heather had stirred and opened her eyes, Rob's were looking back at her. She touched his cheek. She brushed the hair from his forehead, but it fell quickly back, and she laughed.

"What's so funny?"

"Nothing. I just feel happy. That's all."

"No faintness?" he teased. "No palpitations?"

"Not now . . . but last night . . . they were wonderful."

His smile faded. "I do love you, Heather. Do you believe me?"

"I have to now, don't I?"

"Sex and love aren't interchangeable words."

"True," she agreed softly. "But we didn't have sex. . . . You took me against your better judgment last night, didn't you? Your better judgment said that I was tired and that I needed to rest, that I was upset and that it wasn't the right time to make love—"

"But it was the right time. I sat downstairs thinking back on everything that had happened. When I came up here and looked at you, I knew. Making love to you was the only way I could prove to you how much I love you. Yes, ideally I'd have chosen a more romantic time, a time when you were more relaxed and happy, but I'm not sorry it happened. . . . Are you?"

"Do I look sorry?"

He ran a long finger down her cheek and left it to toy with her lips. "You look very, very pretty. And smug. You finally had your way with me, didn't you?"

She gave a wry chuckle. "I'm not sure I did all that much. I was really pretty ignorant . . . about what to do and all."

"You did damn well," he drawled, then winked, "for a beginner."

"You'll have to teach me more."

"I will, dear heart. I will." Quite inadvertently he'd said the one word that could take them both from the cloud they were on. His smile faded, as did hers. "When I came to you last night, I saw that you'd been crying. Why the tears? Was it because you truly believed I'd betrayed your trust?"

She frowned, eyes lowering to the dark swirls of hair on his chest. "I don't think so. You did what you thought was right. I was angry and embarrassed. But . . . it wasn't all that bad. And I do feel relieved in a way."

"And the tears? Honestly."

She raised her eyes to his. "Honestly? The tears were because I was ashamed of the way I'd behaved and the things I said. And I am scared, Rob. I can't deny it."

"From what I saw yesterday, things are pretty optimistic."

"In favor of the operation?"

"If you want it. Yes, the problem should be corrected before you go through a pregnancy, but because you've taken such good care of yourself over the years, the operation would be clear sailing."

"It still scares me. I can't help it—it does."

He curved an encouraging hand around her neck. "That's natural, honey. Operations are scary."

"Did you mean what you said yesterday—that you wouldn't rush me into it?"

"Yes, I mean it. You know that I'm in favor of it. I'd be less than honest if I said anything else. I'm in favor of it because I know you'd do beautifully, and once you have it done, we could go on with our lives."

She gnawed on her lower lip for a minute. "And if I decide to wait a bit? What happens to us then?"

"We can't go back. Not after last night."

"I know that. But will you hold out on me? After last night I'll know what I'll be missing. I don't want to go back to some kind of tease and halt relationship. Will you use lovemaking as a lever to get me to have the operation?"

Rob realized then just how much he'd risked the day before. He truly had dealt a blow to Heather's trust. "No, Heather," he said quietly. "I couldn't do that even if I wanted to, and I don't want to. I don't want anything to mar what we have together. I still want you to marry me. We could do it this weekend if you were willing."

"Why the rush?"

"Because I love you. Because I want you to bear my name and my ring . . ."

"And your children," she whispered, finishing the thought he'd stopped short of airing.

His own whisper was hoarser. "Yes. That, too. Very much."

She swallowed once and looked away from him, but she didn't speak.

"Okay, Heather. What is it? You're thinking something, and I'm not sure what it is. Don't you want to have my children?"

Her eyes flew to his. "Oh, yes! I want your children more than anything in the world."

"But something else is bothering you. Is it to do with the operation?" When she hesitated, he cupped her shoulder. "We have to be honest with each other. If we're going to avoid what happened yesterday, we've got to be honest."

After a minute she nodded. Then her brow furrowed and she avoided his eyes. "I'm supposed to have the operation before I go through a pregnancy. I know that, and you know that. Yesterday when we were talking, I said that there wasn't much chance of my becoming pregnant. That's changed."

Silence hung in the air like a shroud between them. As soon as Rob could muster his thoughts, he sought to push the shroud aside. "And you're wondering if I made love to you purposely to get you to have the operation."

"It's possible. I mean, we didn't use any birth control last night. For all I know I could be pregnant now. And if I am, I'll have no choice but to have your operation."

"It's not my operation, honey. It's yours. I told you that you'd be the one to decide if and when to have it."

"You haven't answered my question."

"No." He rolled onto his back and stared at the ceiling. "It's just . . . I'm trying to straighten out my own thoughts. I didn't think of the possibility of your becoming pregnant. It was stupid of me. I should have used something—not that I had anything with me. I didn't plan on our making love. It was the last thing on my mind when we drove back here yesterday. But I could have withdrawn . . . I could have done something . . . I really didn't think about it." He turned his head on the pillow and looked at her. "Maybe there was something subconscious about what I did, but I swear to God I wasn't aware of it. I know you may not believe me, but it's the truth."

Looking into his eyes, seeing the torment there, she knew it was so. "I believe you. . . . But what do we do now?"

He rolled to his side again and threw an arm around her back. "We wait to see what the story is, and in the meantime we be more careful. I can't stay away from you, Heather. If we had more time now, and if I weren't afraid that you'd be sore, I'd make love to you again." He took her hand, raised it to his lips and kissed it, then guided it steadily down his body. "I want you again. Even after last night, I want you again."

Heather held her breath as her fingers touched the proof of his words. "You're so big . . ." she whispered.

"I was even bigger when I was inside you," he whispered back. "It doesn't frighten you anymore, does it?"

"No. It's a little strange . . . the thought . . . it'll take me a while to believe it really happened. . . ."

He gave a crooked grin. "You'll believe it when you have trouble walking today."

She eyed him defiantly. "I won't have trouble walking."

"Oh, no? Go ahead. Try."

"I will." Throwing back the sheet that had covered them through the night, she swung her legs to the floor, leaned forward to push herself up, then moaned.

Rob would have chuckled had he not been so entranced by the smooth expanse of ivory flesh she'd bared to him. From her shoulders to her bottom, with curves in all the right places, she was lovely.

In a whir of movement, he rolled off the other side of the bed. Heather looked over her shoulder but saw no sign of him. Then she heard quiet grunts interspersed with loud inhalations and exhalations. Stretching across the bed, she peered over the edge to the floor.

Rob was doing push-ups.

8

JASON PARRISH STARED at Rob over lunch in the cafeteria. "You really did that? Tricked her into having the tests?"

"I did."

It was the first time the two men had seen each other in two weeks. Jason had been away at a series of conferences, then had taken a vacation with his family.

"How did she react?"

"Let me tell you, it was touch and go for a while. She was furious with me at first, but she calmed down."

"Then . . . everything's okay?"

"Everything's fine. We're closer now than we've ever been."

"How about medically? What did the tests show?"

"That she should have the operation."

"Will she?"

"I think so . . . in time."

"How much time have you got?"

"Theoretically speaking, all the time in the world. Practically speaking, much less. I want her to marry me, but she refuses to be pinned down to a date. Until we're married, we can't think of having children. She's nearly thirty and I'm nearly forty. The longer we wait, the harder it will be."

"I assume she's using birth control."

Rob's eyes teased him. "You assume much, pal."

"You mean, you're not—"

"We are. And no, she's not using birth control. I am. We sweated it out for a week or two there, but I'm not taking any more chances."

"She trusts you to do it? I'd think you might want to get her pregnant. That way she'd be forced into having the operation."

Rob stared levelly at his friend. "I can't let that happen. I promised her, after what happened with the tests, that I'd let her make the decision on the operation. I think I've finally repaired the harm done to her trust when I went over her head last time. There's no way I'm going to risk blowing it again. By my taking the responsibility for birth control, I can prove to her that I mean what I say. It's a test, in a way."

"And if, by some act of fate, you fail and she becomes pregnant?"

"I'm careful. That won't happen. And even if—by some act of fate, as you put it—it does, she'll know that it wasn't because I didn't try. I mean, it's not like I take a pill in secrecy every night. She sees me put the damn thing on. And, anyway, we're much more open with each other now. I think that even if she did become pregnant we'd be able to talk it out."

"Would she go for the operation if she were pregnant?"

"I think so, yes."

"What's holding her back now?"

"You hit the nail on the head the first time. She's scared, afraid of rocking the boat. She's been doing so well controlling the condition."

"But it has worsened over the years."

"Uh-huh. Not as much as it might have, though. Unfortunately the demands a pregnancy would make on her body would complicate things. Both she and the baby could be in danger."

"What are you doing to convince her to have the operation?"

"Not much. Well, at least not in words. We spend several nights and the weekends together. I'm trying to show her how nice married life would be."

"I take it she equates getting married with having the operation."

Rob nodded. "I haven't pushed, but she's beginning to talk about it more. I've told her that I want to marry her whether she has the operation or not, but she says she wants to be able to come to me as my wife a whole, healthy woman. She's trying to get her nerve up for the operation. She knows the statistics, but she seems fixated on the negative end of the scale. All I can do is reassure her that given the overall state of her health she's got nothing to worry about." He slowly swiveled his head, relaxing the muscles at the back of his neck. "It'll take time, I guess. That's all."

"And in the meantime?"

"I'm taking her down to Bermuda for the heart meetings next week." He smiled, but it was a smile of affection. "She's never flown before. Can you believe that?"

HEATHER CAREFULLY FOLDED a pair of linen shorts and laid them in her suitcase. She was excited . . . phenomenally so. She was flying with Rob to Bermuda, where he'd rented a small house not far from the hotel at which his meetings were being held. She would have the use of the hotel facilities during the day when he was busy. Then they would have the privacy of their own retreat at day's end. She would have the best of both worlds . . . well, in Bermuda, at least.

Gnawing on the inside of one cheek, she glanced back toward the closet. She'd finished the work she'd wanted to get done before the trip. She'd be leaving the next day. If she made the call now, she could promptly forget about it.

Without giving herself further time to think, she crossed the room, dug into the pocket of one of the skirts hanging there and pulled out the piece of paper Rob had given her so many weeks before.

Returning to the bedside phone, she uncrumpled the paper, dialed the number written on it, waited nervously through three rings, then heard the phone picked up. For an instant she debated hanging up. She gripped the receiver more tightly to prevent herself from doing that.

"Hello!" came a breathless, slightly harried-sounding woman's voice on the other end of the line.

"Uh . . . I'd like to speak with Jennifer Gibbons, please."

"Speaking!"

"Jennifer, this is Heather Cole. I was given your name by Robert McCrae—Dr. McCrae—"

"Heather! Dr. McCrae asked me if he could give you my number. I was hoping you'd call. Oh, please hold on a minute!" Her voice came more muffled then. "No, Adam. No. Hot! Come back to Mommy." She spoke directly into the phone again. "I'm sorry, Heather. It's been one of those days."

"How old is your son?"

"Eighteen months, and into everything." Her voice receded. "That's it, sweetheart. Come up on Mommy's lap so I can keep an eye on you while I talk." She grunted, "That's a boy," then returned to Heather. "You'll have to forgive us. As soon as the phone rings, he takes it as license to touch exactly what he's not allowed to touch."

"I'm calling at a bad time. Maybe I should call back later."

"I wouldn't mind talking now—even if this child's absolutely precious, he doesn't exactly stimulate my intellect just yet—but we're bound to have a million interruptions. He takes a good long nap every morning. You could call back tomorrow."

"I'll be going away tomorrow."

"Then—didn't Dr. McCrae say that you live in Chester?"

"Uh-huh."

"I'm in North Branford. It's not far. Why don't you take a ride down now?"

"Oh, I couldn't impose—"

"Don't be silly! It'd be a treat for me. And much easier talking in person than trying to—Adam, sweetheart, you can't chew on the telephone cord—trying to talk this way. Really. I'd love it. If you're free, of course."

Heather knew she needed to talk with someone who was or had been in the same boat she was in now. Before she lost her nerve, succumbed to her cowardice, she accepted the invitation. Around juggling the mischievous Adam on her lap, Jennifer gave her directions. Heather was there within the hour.

Jennifer was pretty in an elfin kind of way. Petite, fair-skinned, she had wispy blond hair and wore large round glasses perched midway down her nose. After offering Heather a drink, she led the way to the back porch of her house, where she put her dark-haired, dark-eyed son in a windup swing and set him in motion.

"Dr. McCrae told me you have the same condition I had."

"That's right.... You say it in the past tense. Is it completely corrected?"

"As completely as anything can be. Oh, I still watch myself. I don't overdo things. But it's amazing—what I consider 'overdoing' now is totally different from what it was before."

"How were you before?"

"Afraid. I pampered myself. So did everyone else. I was living at home because that seemed the safest place to be, and I worked part-time as a bookkeeper because that seemed the quietest thing to do. Then I met Henry."

"Your husband?"

"My husband. He gave me reason to wake up and change my life."

"He wasn't worried about your condition?"

"Oh, yes, he was worried. He was also angry, because he felt I was cheating myself—and him—by refusing to have corrective surgery."

"Why were you refusing it?"

"I was terrified. I hated doctors. I hated hospitals. I'd convinced myself that I was better off going along as I had been—leading a quiet, undemanding life—than taking a chance in the operating room."

"What changed your mind?"

Jennifer tipped her head to the side and frowned. Absently she pushed her glasses higher on her nose. "There were lots of things, I guess, but they all boiled down to Henry. He kept mentioning the things we could do if I wasn't so worried about my heart. He kept talking about the future and about having children."

"He didn't pin a guilt trip on you, did he?"

"With regard to children, no. He was really wonderful. He made it clear that he wanted children because he knew they'd make us both happy, but he was the one who suggested adoption."

"Adoption?" Heather turned to study Adam more closely.

Jennifer joined her in the study, though with pride rather than surprise. "He's from El Salvador," she said, smiling. "We got him eleven months ago, and his arrival couldn't have been timed better."

Heather glanced questioningly back at her, and Jennifer readily explained.

"We really did want children, but I was wary of having the operation that would make it safe. When we began to discuss adopting a child, we realized that there was a scarcity of American babies up for adoption and that if we couldn't have our own it would be nice to have one who really would have been in trouble otherwise. We researched organizations that dealt with Central American countries, chose one, filed applications, filled out God knows how many forms, had interviews and then sat and waited.

"It was as if the pressure were off me then, at least regarding the operation. And without the pressure, I realized how silly I'd been, putting it off." She smiled.

"Adam arrived four months after everything had been corrected, and it's a good thing I'd gone ahead with it. Little did I know then how active he'd come to be." She sent a humorous glance toward her son, who appeared to be falling asleep. "It won't last long. Believe me. This is just a catnap. I'm not the only one he wears out in the course of a day."

Heather looked at the child and smiled. "I'm green with envy. You've got it all worked out."

"Not . . . quite," Jennifer stated with dry good humor, plus something else Heather couldn't put her finger on for a moment. "It appears that I'm pregnant. In seven months I'll have a second little imp to take care of."

That "something else" had been excitement. Heather laughed. "That's wonderful! You and your husband must be thrilled!"

"We are. I may joke about the running around and the work, but I adore Adam and I can't wait for this little one—" she patted her still flat stomach "—to grow. But I've been doing all the talking. Tell me about you, Heather. All Dr. McCrae said was that you were thinking of surgery but that you had many of the same doubts I had."

Heather sipped her iced tea, then set it down on the coaster on the arm of the chair. "I guess that's about where I'm at."

"Are you married?"

"Not yet."

"But there's someone special."

"Very special."

"Is he arguing with you the way Henry did with me?"

"No," Heather answered thoughtfully, "he's really been pretty patient. He's told me how he feels, but he's leaving the final decision up to me."

"Do you want to have children?"

"Very much."

Jennifer leaned forward. "Have the operation, Heather. Maybe I shouldn't be saying that, because I don't know any of the medical details of your case, but I can only tell you what a difference it's made in my own life. I feel free now. I feel normal."

"Was it bad . . . the operation?"

"Not as bad as I'd imagined it would be. I was expecting the worst—pain, complications, outright failure of the procedure. None of them materialized. Sure, I was pretty uncomfortable at first, but medication helps a lot with that. There were no complications, and the procedure itself was a total success."

"No wonder Rob—Dr. McCrae—gave me your name," Heather observed with a wry half grin. "He knew you'd have nothing bad to say."

"But I'd spoken to someone else who had nothing bad to say, and she'd spoken to someone *else* who had nothing bad to say." Jennifer stopped talking and eyed Heather curiously. "Do you know Dr. McCrae personally."

Heather knew that Rob hadn't enlightened Jennifer, but she also knew—he'd been free enough introducing her as his "special lady" to people at the hospital the day she'd taken the tests—that he'd have no objection to Heather's doing so. Jennifer had certainly been forthright enough about herself.

"You might say that I know him personally," Heather said with a full grin this time. "He's the special man I mentioned before."

Jennifer's eyes went wide behind her glasses. "He's the...you mean...Dr. McCrae is...you're going to be marrying..."

"We're trying to work that out. At least, I am. I feel as though I ought to do something about the operation before I finally agree to marry him."

Jennifer was momentarily oblivious to the dilemma Heather broached. "You and Dr. McCrae? That's fantastic! He is the most wonderful man in the world!" She rushed on excitedly. "You can't believe how supportive he was to me. He was there when I went into the operating room, and he was the first one I saw when I came to afterward. I absolutely adore that man. Henry is jealous."

Heather couldn't help but laugh. Jennifer's exuberance was priceless, and it fed her own pride. "But you adore Henry. I'm sure he doesn't have anything to worry about."

"He doesn't now. Wait till I tell him." She leaned forward even more and patted Heather's knee. "That's wonderful, Heather, really wonderful."

"Well," Heather said with a sigh, "it will be if I can get myself straightened out."

"You will. Lord, if I had someone like Dr. McCrae behind me, I wouldn't have a doubt in the world!"

Heather spent another hour talking with Jennifer. Adam woke up in the middle of their conversation, but was temporarily satisfied to sit on his mother's lap and guzzle a baby bottle filled with apple juice. Jennifer

prodded Heather more about her feelings, trying to al-
lay her fears as best she could. In turn, Heather sensed
the openness in the other woman and freely asked questions, some very personal, others more general. By the
time she left, she even knew that Jennifer was planning
to go back to school for a degree in accounting when the
new baby was old enough, and Jennifer knew all about
her handbags. Moreover, Heather promised to drive
down for another visit after she returned from her trip.

BERMUDA WAS THE HONEYMOON before the wedding—at
least that was the way Heather saw it, though she didn't
say it in as many words to Rob. The weather was outstanding, one sunny day after the next. The hotel facilities were luxurious—a huge swimming pool, a beautiful
beach of the smoothest pink sand—and Rob stopped by
to see her at every opportunity.

But the pièce de résistance was the cottage he'd rented.
It was made of rough stone, both inside and out, that
fended off the worst of the heat, while generous windows carried the breeze off the water through the bedroom, kitchen and living room. Sitting on the shore of a
quiet cove, it had a small deck overhanging the water. A
motorboat, moored at its base, was at their disposal.

Heather spent her days at the hotel, her nights with
Rob at the cottage and every dawn on the deck with bin-
oculars pressed to her eyes, spying on a longtail that had
built its nest in a nearby cropping of rocks and was tend-
ing her sweet, round, furry baby bird.

Once, when Rob had a morning free, they rented a
motorbike, and Heather held on while Rob drove them
on a tour of the island. Another time, on a free after-

noon, they strolled arm in arm through downtown Bermuda, browsing in the stores, more interested in each other than in any of the items for sale.

They stayed on for a full day after Rob's meeting ended, and, for Heather, that day was the highlight of the trip. They rented a sailboat, a forty-one-foot Morgan, with a crew and mate to handle the sailing while they basked together on the deck, had cold drinks and cheese in the cockpit, admired the island from the vantage point of the sea and savored the air of freedom that surrounded them.

It was a carefree time, and Heather was grateful for that. For after they returned to Connecticut, "carefree" was but a memory. Rob was snowed under with work, as they'd both known he'd be. Heather herself had a stack of orders waiting to be filled. Dawn and Michael came to visit again, and it seemed that Rob and Heather had precious little time for themselves.

Ten days after their return, she could put it off no longer. She'd driven down to Rob's house for the night. They'd eaten dinner and he was helping her clean up before settling in his den with a briefcaseful of papers. She'd become accustomed to using the time when he worked to do the stitchery she brought along, and although her mind was free enough during those times, his was far from it.

"Rob?"

"Hmm?" He was drying the last of the pots while she sponged off the counters.

She held the sponge suspended above the sink, then slowly set it down. "I'd like you to introduce me to John McHale."

There was a long silence. When she looked up at last, she found that Rob, too, had stopped what he was doing. He was staring at her wide-eyed, whether disbelieving or pleased, she didn't know. So she blinked and went on very, very quietly.

"I think it's about time."

"You want to discuss the operation," he said nearly as quietly.

"Yes. You said he was the best man to do it."

"He is!" Then more softly, "He is."

"Will you make an appointment for me, or should I call him myself?"

Rob tried to contain his relief—and pleasure. He didn't want to come across sounding victorious. "I'll call him to explain the situation and let him know you'll be contacting him, but I think you should set up the appointment yourself."

She nodded. "Will you do it tomorrow?"

"I can . . . if that's what you'd like."

"It is. I've made up my mind."

"To go ahead and have the operation?"

He would never have caught her hesitation had he not been looking directly into her eyes. It was subtle and gone in a split second. "Yes."

He felt impelled to probe her feelings. "Why, honey?"

"Because it does need to be done."

"But you've known that all along."

"Not . . . entirely." She looked down at the sink. "If I'd continued living the way I had been before I met you, I might never have had it done—at least, not unless my condition suddenly worsened. I always knew that it would have to be done if I wanted to have children, but

I was never really sure that would happen. I mean, I wanted to have children, but, as you said—" she blushed "—I needed a man before that could happen." Her eyes met his. "I told you once that I might have put off forming relationships because it would be unfair to whatever man I met. There's another side to that. Maybe subconsciously I didn't want to face the prospect of having children because of the operation. I don't know. If I was torn inside, I didn't think about it. I took things one day at a time."

She paused for just a minute, and Rob didn't rush her. He wanted her to say everything that was on her mind.

"Then I met you," she continued, "and everything happened and . . . well, taking life one day at a time isn't enough. You've made me look toward the future. I can't picture a future without you. And I can't picture a future without our children." She gave a shaky sigh. "So I guess that future is going to have to include the operation, right?"

Rob set the pan and cloth on the counter. Draping his arm around Heather's shoulder, he began to lead her out to the deck.

"You've got work to do," she reminded him softly.

"My work will wait. Nothing's more important than this." He set her in a deck chair and pulled one over for himself. "You're very nervous about it, aren't you?"

"The operation? Yes."

"But you really have made up your mind."

"Yes. . . . I've been in touch with Jennifer Gibbons."

Rob's jaw dropped. "You have? I thought you'd long since thrown away her name and number!"

"No. The piece of paper has been where I put it in the pocket of my skirt all along. I haven't worn that skirt since the day you gave me the paper. I kept looking at the skirt, knowing I should call Jennifer but putting it off. I finally got up my nerve the day before we left for Bermuda."

"You did!" He was pleased, and that pleased her.

"Uh-huh. As a matter of fact, I drove down to see her that afternoon."

"You didn't tell me."

"Obviously," she drawled, then explained. "I had to think about what she'd said. I've spoken with her several times since we've been back. She's a wonderful woman. She adores you."

"Naturally," Rob teased, ducking his head.

"We've really become friends."

"With a capital 'F'?"

Heather breathed a laugh. "Getting there. It's a relief to be able to talk with someone who's gone through the same things. She's very optimistic...but, then, you knew she would be, didn't you?"

"Guilty as charged," he said, and simply shrugged. "As a matter of fact, I think she's coming in for an appointment next week. I'm not sure why. I've been in touch with her personal doctor and she's in fine health."

Heather knew why Jennifer was going to see Rob. "She's pregnant."

"Is that so!" he exclaimed in delight. "That would explain it, then. Not that she's got a thing to worry about, but often patients just want to hear it from me."

"She's really excited about the baby, but she's also got her hands full with the one she already has. You know about Adam, don't you?"

"Sure. Jennifer was in for a routine follow-up two months after she and Henry got him. Adorable kid."

"I know.... He got me thinking, too. There are so many couples in this world who desperately want kids and can't have them. They go for tests. Sometimes the women have surgery and still don't conceive. So they fill out adoption papers and wait and wait. Somehow, when I think about what they go through, I realize that this operation may be a relatively small price to pay for having a child." She shook her head in amazement. "Jennifer's so happy. She's got it all behind her. I want that, too."

Rob bent closer. "And you'll have it. You'll have it all! Hey, it may be that you won't conceive right off the bat, either, but that's got nothing to do with your heart condition, and to tell you the truth, there's so much I want to do with you that I wouldn't mind if we waited a little while before having kids. I want you to travel with me more. Once we're parents, we'll have to worry about baby-sitters."

Heather smiled. "I loved Bermuda, Rob. I loved flying and motorbiking and sailing. I'd love to do more things like that."

"You will!"

"But Bermuda got me thinking, too—about having the operation," she said more cautiously. "Meeting your colleagues was ... wonderful. I'm so proud of you and I feel proud to be with you. But meeting your friends in an island paradise was one thing." She frowned, trying to find the words to express what she wanted to say. "It was unreal, removed from reality—reality being the hospital. If I were to meet your friends in New Haven now, I'd see the hospital looming all around, and I'd probably be uncomfortable. I don't want it to be that way. I want to meet the people you talk about—Howard and Jason and the others. I want to be able to stop by in the middle of the day and meet you for lunch without being nervous."

"Even after the operation you're apt to make some negative associations," Rob cautioned. "Ingrained, perhaps, but they may linger."

"But if the operation's behind me, I'll be able to handle them and get over them. I want us to be able to entertain people from the hospital or the med school or colleagues of yours from different parts of the country, and I want to enjoy it. I want *you* to be able to enjoy it without being afraid that I'll wither up in fear."

"You won't 'wither up in fear,'" he scoffed playfully.

"You haven't wanted to upset me, so you've minimized any contact I've had to have with the hospital, haven't you? Be honest."

"I guess...maybe I have." He'd been momentarily put on the spot, so he'd yielded. He went on to play devil's advocate. "But you know that I'll take you places with me whether or not you have that operation. You could have marriage, too, and we could adopt kids. In a sense, you've got everything now."

She was shaking her head, inhaling deeply. "I don't have the self-image that I want, that I need. Bermuda helped me see that, too. When we were down there I felt like another person. It was an entirely new place for me, a new experience. I felt whole and healthy. The instant we touched down in New York I felt different."

"You're still whole and healthy—"

"Relatively whole and relatively healthy. More to the point, though, I saw myself again as I've seen myself all my life. I returned to the same image I've held for years, and after being free of that image for five days, it was a shock. I don't want that image anymore, Rob. I want to change it."

"You told me that you've never really brooded about your heart condition."

"Not consciously. It just became...part of me, I guess. Looking back now, I think I was always aware of this *thing* hovering over my head. I got used to it and learned to live with it, so I honestly didn't consciously think about it often. When I did think about it, I was frightened, and . . . I think maybe the fear was built into something unrealistic over the years."

"Jennifer has helped you see that?"

"Maybe. Maybe I'm just tired of being afraid. I want it done. I'm willing to take the risk to put it behind me."

Rob put his elbows on his spread knees and reached for her hand. He ran his thumb over its back. "As long as you're sure," he said quietly.

Puzzled, she studied him. "I'd have thought you'd be happy. You don't seem it."

"I am happy."

"But you've just given me all the reasons I don't need to have the operation. I don't understand."

He raised his eyes to hers then. They were dark gray and intense. "There's one part of me that's afraid, too— not about the operation," he rushed to add when he saw her catch her breath, "because I've got every faith that it will go smoothly."

"What are you afraid of?" she whispered urgently.

He frowned and thought, then spoke. "I want to be sure—I want you to be sure—that this is what *you* want. I don't want you to be making this decision because of me. I've been in favor of surgery from the beginning. We both know that, and it hasn't changed. I'm still in favor of it—for all the reasons you've given now and then some. But I'm worried, afraid that maybe I've influenced you too strongly."

It was Heather's turn to lean forward, until her face was inches from his. She curved her free hand around his neck. "Yes, you've influenced me strongly, but not 'too' strongly, and not wrongly. Everything you've said from the first has been right. It's only now that I can admit it to myself, and to you." Her voice grew exquisitely soft. "I love you, Rob. If I'd never met you, probably none of this would be happening, but so much of it is healthy and right and wonderful that I wouldn't have it any other way. I'm having this operation for you, because I know you want to marry me and you want me to have your children. But more important, I'm having it for me, because I want all those things and more! I want a future, Rob, a nice, bright, boundless future. I want it." She squeezed his neck and whispered a broken, "I want it."

Rob pulled her onto his lap and held her tightly for a long, long time. They'd said all that needed to be said on the subject at that moment. Well, nearly all. "I love you, Heather. I can never say it enough, but when you talk with me the way you have tonight, even the words seem inadequate." He let it go at that, because indeed words did seem inadequate.

He didn't step foot into his den that night.

THE NEXT DAYS went by in a whir for Heather. With Rob by her side, she met with John McHale, who explained the specifics of the operation to her. She had several additional tests, which John had wanted to run, and between those results and the ones from Rob's original examination and tests, John agreed that her prognosis was excellent. The operation, being elective, was scheduled for two weeks from then. The prospect of the wait was a source of dismay for Heather, though she knew the delay would have been even longer had not both Rob and John carried heavy weight at the hospital.

As it turned out, she had barely enough time to build up her supply of handbags to counter the period when she wouldn't be able to work. When she called Elaine Miller to explain the situation, Elaine was furious at her for not having mentioned her condition sooner.

"And here I've been piling you with orders!" she berated herself after she'd finished chastising Heather.

"But I'm fine, Elaine, and I have been all along. This is a chronic condition that I'm finally getting around to taking care of."

"Thanks goodness for that. Listen, don't worry about a thing. You say you'll be getting that last bunch of bags to me by the end of the week?"

"By hook or by crook."

"Well, you do it, and then forget about it. When you're feeling comfortable and strong after the operation, you

can think of starting up again. It'll do the stores good to
be champing at the bit for a while."

"You'll keep them champing?" Heather asked. It had
occurred to her that in her absence some of the stores
might find superior substitutes.

"You bet. And if you need anything, *anything*, you
give me a call. Got that?"

Heather smiled. "I do. And thanks, Elaine."

"Hey, what are friends for, anyway?"

Friends were for, among other things, giving support,
and Heather's other friends rose to the occasion. Beth
Windsor stopped by the house several times a week to
make sure Heather's spirits were high. Sally Schein, the
neighbor whose son had broken his leg, not only offered
to check the house every day while Heather was in the
hospital, but promptly began to cook double portions
of things and freeze half so that Heather wouldn't have
to worry about cooking for days after the operation. She
was nearly as conscious of nutrition as Heather was, and
they'd always compared and shared recipes.

Jennifer proved to be a friend, indeed, driving up to
Chester several times during those two weeks. She knew
what it was to wait, to anticipate, to fear, and she spent
hours talking with Heather, assuring her and reassuring
her, indulgently answering her questions a second, then
a third time, while Heather kept her hands busy at her
work. Adam, mercifully, was thoroughly preoccupied
with scraps of fabric, ends of yarn and beads Heather had
deemed large enough to let him play with safely.

Rob, though, was the most supportive at all. They
spent every night together, either at her house or his, and
he called her at least once during the day. He could eas-

ily detect those moments when she grew apprehensive, when her brow would furrow even momentarily or her hands would be less than steady. He would speak in his most gentle voice at those times, giving her encouragement, telling her how proud he was of her, how confident, how much he loved her.

It was his love she was thinking of when she checked into the hospital that Tuesday afternoon in early October, and again when she was given a sedative that night, and still again when she was prepared for surgery very early the next morning. Rob was there to remind her of it when she grew logy under the effect of the preoperative medication. It was the last thought she had before she was put fully to sleep.

9

THE OPERATION went as smoothly as Rob had assured
Heather it would. She awoke very groggy in the recovery room, then was taken to the coronary care unit,
where she remained for two days before being trans-
ferred to a private room.

Rob spent every free minute with her, stopping in between appointments, meetings and office time. He was
there when she awoke in the morning and was with her
when she fell asleep at night. For hours he sat by her
bedside, holding her hand while she lay quietly, working at the bedside stand while she dozed. He talked softly,
adjusted her bed or the headphones of her small cassette
recorder, turned the television on or off. He praised both
her courage and her progress, and never tired of telling
her how much he loved her.

The first few days were the most uncomfortable for
her. Her chest hurt inside and out, and though the pain-
killers she was given helped, they couldn't provide total
relief. She didn't mind the leads to the heart monitor that
were taped to her, but she could have done without the
intravenous needle in her hand and the respirator tube
down her throat. The latter came out after a day, the IV
after two. Within thirty-six hours of the operation she
was taking liquids, and Rob and the nurses conspired to

get her dangling her feet over the side of the bed, then walking as much as possible.

For the most part she was a good patient. Though Rob could sense when something was bothering her, she complained very little. If she was moody from time to time, taken to lying silently in bed, he understood. He'd seen too many patients recovering from open heart surgery to be deeply concerned.

Her largest problem became one of confidence in the artificial valve that had replaced her own diseased one. She was wary of moving too much for fear of straining something. Though Jennifer had warned her that she'd feel this way, forewarned was not forearmed. Despite the assurances that Rob, John and the residents and nurses gave her, she had trouble adjusting to the idea of something foreign being dependable.

Five days after the operation she awoke from a midafternoon nap knowing that something was different. She lay still for a minute, then looked around the room. Gingerly she shifted her legs; they worked fine. She looked down at her chest, then raised her right hand to the spot on her hospital gown beneath which bandages covered her incision. The dressing was the same. But her hand... not the right but the left hand... an odd sensation... yet the IV had been out for several days. She lifted that hand, then caught her breath and stared. Slowly she smiled, and for an instant her eyes grew moist. Less slowly, but wincing at the movement, she reached to press the button for the nurse.

"I need to see Dr. McCrae," she announced excitedly when the figure in white appeared at her door.

The nurse came quickly forward, well aware that Heather was a VIP of sorts. "Is something wrong? Would you like medication?"

Heather had her left hand tucked protectively in her right. "No. No medication. Just Rob. Quickly."

"Are you sure there isn't anything *I* can get you?" the nurse asked anxiously. The last thing she wanted was for Heather to report to Dr. McCrae that she'd been ignored. Not that it was the case—or that Heather seemed like the kind of woman to complain even if it were so— but a doctor of Robert McCrae's status was not to be offended.

"Just Rob," Heather repeated.

The nurse headed back toward the door. "I'm not sure exactly where he is. I'll have him paged. It may take a few minutes, though."

Five minutes later Rob rushed into Heather's room. His eyes were wide in alarm. "What is it, honey?"

Throat tight, she simply held out her arms, then wrapped them around him when he came close. "I was sleeping," she managed hoarsely. "How could you just slip it on when I was sleeping, when I couldn't tell you how beautiful it was and how happy I am and how much I love you?"

Rob released a ragged breath into her hair. "Oh, God, I thought something was wrong! They didn't say what it was when they paged me. I left a patient smack in the middle of an exam."

"I had to see you.... I'm sorry."

He drew his head back, then kissed her gently. The lines of tension eased from his face, and for the first time since he'd entered the room, he smiled. "Don't be sorry. This was the nicest scare I've had in months."

Heather raised the sparkling diamond so they could both see it. "It's magnificent, Rob. Thank you."

"Just so you know that we are getting married. You've got no excuse to put me off any longer."

"You'll have to wait till I get back on my feet. I want to plan a pretty wedding, and I want to feel strong."

"You're getting there fast."

"I've . . . still got a ways to go."

He stroked her hair, gentling its waves. He knew she was discouraged, though medically she had no right to be. He'd had the diamond for over a month and had felt that giving it to her now would be a boost to her morale. Judging from the hesitation in her voice in that instant, he wasn't sure if it would prove to be so, but not for a minute did he regret formalizing their engagement. He gave her a tender smile, lifted her hand and kissed it, then gently kissed her lips.

"You'd better rest and gain that strength, then. I'm not waiting for long. But my patient is. Poor Mr. Pugach. I'd better run. I'll be in to see you a little later."

She wished he could stay now. She felt most secure when he was with her. But she simply nodded and gave what she thought to be a brave smile. "Later."

Though Heather was thrilled with the ring and looked at it constantly, she couldn't seem to focus on the future when so much of her effort was taken with worry about whether her repaired heart would get her safely down the hall and back the next time she was forced to make the trip. She refused to believe that the valve would work and refused to see that she was truly gaining strength from one day to the next.

Rob's friends were wonderful. Howard Cerillo stopped by each day, taking delight in instructing her to call him if Rob got troublesome in any way. Jason Parrish visited several times during her stay and repeatedly, if gently, urged her to call him if anything was bothering her that she wanted to discuss.

Elaine came to visit, bringing a magnificent batiste nightgown and robe set. Beth Windsor came by with an armload of the latest best-sellers she'd received at her store. Sally Schein stole in with a chicken, walnut and grape salad she'd made, plus a thermos of apple cider, compliments of Ruth Babcock.

Jennifer Gibbons came. She brought only Henry. It was for Heather the nicest visit of all.

Ten days after surgery, she left the hospital. Though in one of her testier moments she'd insisted that she wanted to go to Chester, Rob was able to convince her that their original plan for her to recuperate at his home in Woodbridge, from which he could commute that much more easily, was the wiser one. He'd hired a nurse to be with her during those times when he had to be at the hospital, but he came home to have lunch with her every day.

During those first two weeks home, she spent most of her time resting, listening to music, reading the newspaper or a book. She spoke with Jennifer on the phone and received calls from other friends, but she hated to tie the line up lest Rob should be trying to get through. Though the nurse he'd hired provided her with everything she needed, she counted the minutes until he walked through the front door. Only then could she relax a little.

When she expressed anxiety about being alone, Rob readily retained the nurse for a third week. By the fourth, though, there was no practical reason for the woman to remain. Heather had been checked out back at the hospital both by Rob and John and had been given a glowing physical report. Her incision had healed nicely; her heart was stronger than ever, and she was cleared—and encouraged—to be up and about at will.

That fourth week was the hardest for Heather, since she was alone so much of the time. She began to cook, though the freezer was stocked with the goodies Sally had delivered, and upon Rob's firm instruction—he demanded a report at the end of each day—she was bundling up against the November chill and taking short walks in the yard. When he suggested that he bring her sewing machine down from Chester, though, she shook her head, saying that she didn't feel up to working yet.

Emotionally her days followed a pattern. Each morning she anxiously kissed Rob goodbye at the door, standing there, watching plaintively until his car was out of sight. Then she passed the morning in one quiet activity or another, always with her eye on the phone, waiting for the minute when he'd call and she'd feel more secure. He continued to join her for lunch that first week after the nurse left, and she clung to his hand whenever it was free, dreading the moment when he'd have to return to the hospital. The happiest times were when he came home at night, for she knew that she'd have nearly twelve straight hours of safety. She didn't mind that he spent hours in his den each night to compensate for his having left the hospital earlier than he might have otherwise; she curled up on the sofa and relaxed, only having to glance his way to remind herself that he was there should anything go wrong.

Nothing went wrong, at least not physically. But Rob began to urge her to do more, and they inevitably argued. When he suggested they spend the weekend on Cape Cod, she vetoed the idea on the grounds that she wasn't up to a four-hour drive. When he modified the plan and suggested a night in New York City, she cowered at the thought of the crowds and noise. When he suggested that they go to a movie, she opted for watching one on television.

"You can't stay around here forever," he said with a weary sigh.

"We'll get out. I just need a little more time."

"Who says that? Not John. Not me. And we're the ones who should know."

"I'm the one who should know. It's my body. Besides, it's cold outside."

"That's what down parkas are made for. The cold air won't hurt you."

"I've read that it can be a shock to the system and that anyone with a heart condition should avoid it."

"Right, if you happen to be a seventy-five-year old who's had two major heart attacks and it's ten degrees outside with a windchill factor of thirty below. Come on, Heather. You're using the cold as an excuse."

"I'm trying to be reasonable! Is that a crime?"

It wasn't a crime, but, then, neither was she being reasonable, Rob knew. He grew more and more discouraged as the days passed and the situation didn't improve.

When he gradually began to wean her off his lunchtime visits—he felt he was losing valuable time racing back and forth to Woodbridge, time he'd rather spend with her at night—she seemed so downtrodden that he felt guilty and in turn angry. He still called her several times during the course of the day, and each time she picked up the phone before it barely had a chance to ring. He suspected that she positioned herself right next to the instrument and spent most of the day waiting for it to sound. On one occasion there was an evening dinner meeting that, for professional reasons, he simply couldn't miss. When he told Heather he wouldn't be home until late, she looked as though she'd lost her best friend.

The Heather he'd fallen in love with had been reduced to a woman who was afraid of her own shadow. Even in bed—lovemaking had been okayed after her last exam—she held back, as though to yield to pleasure and passion would be inviting heart failure.

Not sure what to do, Rob called Jennifer—as a friend, rather than a doctor—and enlisted the help that she was more than glad to give. The very next day she left Adam with a sitter and popped in to visit Heather.

"You've got to work," she announced firmly. She knew Heather wouldn't be offended by her forwardness. They'd become too close friends for that.

Heather gave a lopsided grin. "Why do I have to work?"

"Because you're stagnating."

"I'm not stagnating. I read. I cook. I rest."

"You're in limbo. You've got to pick up your life and move on with it."

"I will."

"When?"

"Soon."

"Heather, it's been seven weeks since the operation! What are you waiting for?"

"I'm waiting to feel stronger. You, of all people, should understand that."

"You bet I do. I know that I felt very much the same way until we got the call that Adam would be coming. In one day's time—so help me God, one day—I was miraculously cured. I completely forgot about the aches and pains. Okay, you haven't got an Adam on the way. But you've got your work, which would take your mind off your body. Those stores need bags."

"I've been supplying them with fall things since July."

"But you haven't given them anything in a while. They've probably sold what they've got and are waiting for more. What does Elaine say?"

"That they're waiting for more. But she's not rushing me."

"She should. Maybe I'll give her a call."

"Don't you dare."

Jennifer, who'd been standing directly before Heather, sat beside her on the sofa. "You're fine now. Physically, you're fine. Emotionally, you've still got a problem, and that particular stenosis is worsening." She took a deep breath. "Heather, I care about you, and I'm concerned. Imagine what Rob's feeling."

"Rob's okay."

"But he's used to seeing a woman who *does* something with her life. Now he has to go to work and leave you here to twiddle your thumbs. He must feel guilty as sin."

Heather looked down. "He doesn't."

"You're angry at him."

"No ..."

"You're angry that he isn't here with you. I was angry at Henry when he had to go to work. But how can Rob be here, Heather? He's got so many responsibilities at the hospital. He's trying to divide his time sensibly. When you were really ill at first, he was with you more. But you're not ill anymore. And there are so many people who are, people he owes his care to. He can't in good conscience sit here with you when you don't need him to do that."

"I do need him," Heather said in a meeker voice. "I don't feel comfortable when he's not here."

Jennifer sat back on the sofa. "What you're experiencing is very common. While we're in the hospital, we've got any number of people seeing to our well-being. It's a shock when we get home, when all of a sudden we don't have that cadre of support. It's like having the rug pulled from under our feet. Most of us have to straighten ourselves out pretty quick. We don't have any other choice. The problem here is that you have had a choice, Rob being a doctor, your doctor, and all. You've heard of female patients having crushes on their doctors? Well, it's mainly a part of that dependency syndrome. A patient's doctor, more than anyone else, is representative of security."

"I don't have a crush on Rob."

"Of course not. You love him. And you did before all this happened, but that doesn't mean you're any less dependent on him. You weren't always that way, were you?"

"I always looked forward to seeing him. I've always been happiest when I was with him."

"But . . . dependent?"

"I can't help it if I rely on him. Isn't that what love's all about?"

"It's one of the things. But there are others."

"I'm not sure what you're trying to tell me, Jen."

Jennifer shoved up her glasses. "I'm saying that you've got to stop being a patient and start being a person again, and one way of doing that is to go back to work. Even aside from any consideration of Rob, you owe it to yourself to move ahead. You're well enough to do it. Rob's told you so. Your surgeon's told you so. You may be hesitant, but you'll still be hesitant in a month, or two, or four. The only way to convince yourself that you're well is to show yourself that you're well. Build up your confidence slowly. Take it one day at a time. Plan something new to do each day, something a little more challenging than what you did the day before. It'll work, Heather. Believe me, it'll work."

Bolstered by Jennifer's pep talk, Heather let Rob cart her sewing machine, plus a supply of materials, from Chester to Woodbridge. He set her up in one of the spare rooms, and was pleased to see her there for reasons above and beyond those dealing with her health.

Unfortunately she didn't accomplish much. At the end of each day he'd ask how she'd done, only to find that she'd had trouble with one pattern or another, or that she'd torn out some beadwork when she'd been dissatisfied with it, or simply that she'd tired early and had put the work away.

She continued to be at the door when he left, then again, waiting, when he returned. She continued to snatch the phone up when he called, then to prolong the conversation, as though something terrible would happen to her when it ended. Though she'd reluctantly released him from rushing home to lunch with her, she continued to be disappointed whenever he had an evening meeting or if he left for the hospital a minute earlier in the morning.

It was with great trepidation that, after procrastinating as long as possible, Rob broke the news that he had to fly to an intensive two-day seminar in Minneapolis. They were eating breakfast at the time, and it was three days before he was due to leave.

"Minneapolis? But . . . but that's so far away!"

"Not as the crow or the plane flies," he quipped, trying to make light of the trip when he could see sheer terror in Heather's eyes.

"Do you have to go?" she pleaded.

"Yes. It's a training session on a new diagnostic procedure. I'm New Haven's sole representative."

"Couldn't Howard go . . . or someone else?"

"I'm the chief of cardiology. I have to go. I want to go. This is what my career's about. I thought of taking you along with me, but it won't be like Bermuda. Minneapolis is cold, really cold this time of year, and there'd be nothing for you to do but sit in a hotel room and wait." In truth, though he hated to admit it, he needed a break. He was tired of feeling guilty when he had to work, and he couldn't bear the thought of rushing back to a hotel room to coddle Heather.

"But . . . but what will I do while you're gone?"

He put down his fork. He'd only been picking at his eggs, anyway. "The same things you've been doing here."

"But I'll be alone."

"There's nothing wrong with that," he said, trying to curb his impatience. "It's only for one night, Heather."

She pushed herself from the table and stalked to the sink. "One night can be an eternity! I don't want you to go, Rob."

"I have to."

She whirled around. "You don't. You could send someone else."

"I've already told you," he gritted. "I can't do that."

"You don't want to do it."

"For God's sake, Heather!" he exploded. The feelings had built up in him for so long that he simply lost control. "I've rearranged my entire schedule for weeks now so that I could be with you as much as possible. Whenever I can, I stay here a little later in the mornings and come home a little earlier at night. I rush through rounds like a house afire. I have other doctors covering for me right and left, not to mention rearranging their own schedules to meet with me at my convenience. I'm exhausted because I'm up till all hours doing the work I should have done at the hospital—not that there's any reason for me to come to bed. Whenever we make love, you're stiff as a board." His words had escaped in anger, but he wasn't sorry he'd said them. They were the truth. Maybe it was time he confronted her. At least, that was what Jason had told him, albeit not in relation to sex, when they'd talked earlier that week.

Heather was duly stung. She lashed out in self-defense. "My chest is still sore."

"Not very," he countered, eyes sharp. "And not when you're flat on your back."

"That's crude."

"It's the truth. Think about it. You've got yourself convinced that if you let yourself go you'll break into little pieces. Well, you won't, Heather! There's nothing wrong with you now! It's all psychological!"

"You're saying I have an emotional problem."

"That's exactly what I'm saying. You're hung up on something that's absurd. You're fine now. When are you going to start believing it?"

"Maybe if you were around more to convince me, I would."

He threw up his hands. "My God, I can't be around any more than I am. I don't know how you can stand being here day in and day out. I'd go stark raving mad!" He rose from the table, pushing his chair back as he stood. Its legs grated against the floor. "And don't say that I haven't offered to take you out, because I have. You won't go anywhere!"

"I'm more comfortable here. And I thought you enjoyed my company. I hadn't realized you've been so dissatisfied."

Hearing her hurt, Rob made an effort to soften his tone. "I wouldn't be dissatisfied if you'd snap out of this self-indulgent funk you're in." He raked a heedless hand through his still damp, freshly combed hair. "I'm doing everything I can to help you. I just don't know what to do next. What do you want from me?"

Her lower lip trembled. "I want your company."

"You have it, at least as much as I can possibly give you."

"But I need more."

It was starting again. They were going in circles. "Well, maybe I need more, too," he said tightly. "Maybe I need a little bit of strength from you every so often. I feel like I'm walking on eggshells around here, because it's inevitable that I go to work and I know that upsets you. I haven't even dared mention marriage again—you get all hesitant and vague. Let me tell you, Heather, no one likes being put on hold time after time after time." He stuck his hands on his hips. "You do want to marry me, don't you? Or was I mistaken about that, too?"

"You're having second thoughts," she cried fearfully.

He took a deep breath and approached her. "Heather, my God, stop and listen to yourself. You sound totally insecure, and when you harp on my being here you sound possessive. You practically hang on me!"

"You used to like it."

"That was when you wanted to do it. Now you need to. There's a difference."

"And you can't understand my need?"

"No, I can't. I've tried, and for a long time I did understand, but it's no good anymore. It's gone on too long. You're stifling me, and you're stifling yourself."

"You don't love me anymore."

"I love the woman you were and the woman you can be. No, I don't love the woman who invalids herself unnecessarily. Think about it, Heather. Stand back and take a good look at what you've done to yourself.... Ah, hell, I have to get out of here."

Without another word, he strode from the kitchen, snatched up his blazer, topcoat and briefcase and stormed out the front door. Heather stood at the kitchen sink, listening to the sound of his car as it wheeled from the drive. Then, trembling, she broke down and cried.

"JASON? It's Heather Cole."

"Heather! How are you?"

"Uh, not so good. I...I wonder if I could...could talk with you."

"Are you feeling all right?"

"Physically... yes."

"But you sound upset."

"You said I should call if . . . anything was bothering me."

"I'm glad you have.... Listen, I can get away from here in about twenty minutes. If you fix me a sandwich for lunch, we can talk while we eat. Sound fair?"

"Sounds fair."

Jason was all too willing to make a house call. He knew how discouraged Rob was with Heather's behavior, also knew that Heather would have to be very upset to call him. His original offer had been a sincere one, but he'd never expected her to take him up on it. He was happy that she had, both for her sake and for Rob's.

She met him at the door, looking pretty, though pale. He could see she'd been crying.

"Thank you for coming," she said softly. Her eyes held apology and a certain amount of timidity.

Jason stepped forward and gave her a gentle hug. He would have done so purely because she was the woman his good friend loved, but he was additionally inspired because she looked so lost and lonely. He wanted her to know that he was her friend. "Anytime. I told you that."

She let herself relax against him for a minute before taking her own weight again. "I made you a sandwich—chicken and avocado. Is that okay?"

He smiled. "Very interesting. Lead the way."

Moments later they were in the semicircular eating area of the kitchen. He waited until she'd poured hot tea and joined him at the table. Then he said softly, "Talk to me, Heather."

It took her a minute to find the courage to begin. She studied her teacup, then wrapped her hands around it in search of warmth. "Rob and I argued this morning. We've argued before, but he's never said things as bluntly as he did today." Her voice shook lightly. "Some of what he said really hurt, and it scared me and made me look at myself, and that scared me all the more." She raised confused eyes to Jason, whose own were gentle and understanding and gave her the encouragement she needed.

"Since the operation I've become a different person. I thought I'd be so relieved to have it over and to know that I was cured, but it hasn't worked that way. I'm more frightened now than I ever was. I can't seem to get myself going, and I don't understand it." Her eyes grew moist, so she lowered them and swallowed to ease the tightness in her throat. "What's wrong with me, Jason?" she whispered.

He spoke very softly. "You're going through a very natural period of adjustment."

"But it should be over by now. At least, that's what everyone says. I should be back to doing what I was before and then some, but I feel paralyzed. I . . . I didn't know that it bothered Rob so, not until this morning. He was so angry and disgusted. I don't think he respects me anymore. I'm not even sure he still loves me."

"He still loves you. More than ever. That's why he was so angry. And if he sounded disgusted, it was probably with himself."

"But why would he be disgusted with himself, when he's got every right to be disgusted with me?"

"Because he realizes that he's been party to your problems, and now he's got to try to turn that around, and it hurts."

She frowned. "I don't understand."

"You had major surgery, and it's understandable that you'd be a while getting back on your feet. Rob coddled you—more than was necessary at first—but his love is such that he couldn't help himself. He gave you a crutch to lean on, without realizing that it would keep you from walking on your own. Now he sees what he's done and he's disgusted with himself. Yes, maybe he's disgusted with you, too, for having let him do it, but that doesn't mean he doesn't love you anymore."

"*I* don't love me anymore," she cried. "He was right when he told me to take a good look at what I've become. I don't like what I see. How can *he* possibly like it?"

"He remembers you as you were before. He knows what you can be again. What you heard from him this morning was frustration. He simply doesn't know what to do to help you. So he got angry. Maybe he was trying

to shock you into taking action on your own. It sometimes takes a shock in this kind of situation."

Heather recalled Jennifer's saying that for her it took
the announcement of the baby's imminent arrival. Perhaps Jason was right. He ought to know. "But I still feel
scared. I feel…I feel as though as long as someone's here
with me I'm okay. You're here now, so it's a little better.
When Rob's here, I'm okay. The thought of being alone
with this . . . this thing—"

"The artificial valve?"

She nodded. "I don't trust it."

"Even after seven weeks of perfect performance? Even
with thousands and thousands of people having bene-
fitted from similar valves and artificial parts?" He
reached over and clasped her forearm. "You've got to
stop listening to that tiny hysterical voice inside and start
listening to the messages your body's been sending for
weeks now. The hysterical voice is exactly that. Hysterical. It's highly emotional. It doesn't know the facts, and
it's preventing you from seeing and believing them."

She was watching him, listening closely, so he went on.
"Rob's told you the facts. So has John, I'm sure. Your
heart is functioning beautifully. You're well. Tell me
honestly. Do you feel weak? Is there anything physically
that feels wrong?"

"My chest still hurts sometimes."

"A pinch here, a twinge there. But less with each passing day. Am I right?"

"I guess so."

"Try again. Concentrate on your body. Do you, right
now, feel that it's not functioning properly?"

There was a moment of silence. "No…."

"Once more. Without the hesitation this time. Do you feel physically ill?"

"No."

He sat back. "Good. That's the first step in your recovery." They both knew that the recovery he was referring to was the emotional one. "That's what you've got to focus on when you find yourself getting anxious."

"But I do get anxious! I can't help myself!"

"You can conquer it if you want to.... Do you want to?"

"I want Rob to love me again."

"Rob loves you now."

"I want him to respect me again."

"What about you?"

She answered very quietly. "Yes, I want to respect myself."

"Okay. There's the second step in your recovery. You have to want it in order for it to happen."

"But...where to I go from here? What's the third step?"

Jason regarded her more thoughtfully. "I can make a recommendation, but I'm not sure you'll like it."

"Please, Jason. I need help!"

"That may be the third step right there—the realization that you do need help. And since I'm here, you've already taken that step."

"And . . . your recommendation?"

He raised both brows, then lowered them and took a breath. "I think you should go back to Chester. Alone."

"Alone! But . . ."

"You can't make it alone? Of course you can. You did it for...how many years? And with a shaky heart at that. But your heart's been fixed. It's not shaky anymore.

Think about it. You're in much better shape than you were before, and you were living alone then. Am I right?"

Subdued, she replied, "I've never thought about it that way."

"But it's true, Heather. You're safer alone in Chester now than you were before."

"The words sound right. Believing them is something else."

"The proof of the pudding is in the eating."

She pondered that for a minute. Hadn't Jennifer said something similar? "Maybe I could just start doing more here."

"You could, but it wouldn't be the same. You need to prove to yourself—and to Rob—that you can be as independent, as self-sufficient as you always were."

"But Chester is so . . . far away. If something happened—"

He was shaking his head with such confidence that she had to listen to what he was saying. "Nothing's going to happen. Besides, Chester wasn't so far away before. You chose to live there, diseased valve and all. You'd be going back with a valve that's fully repaired. You'd be able to pick up where you left off, then zip ahead."

In spite of that tiny hysterical voice, she found something appealing in that prospect. "But . . . what about Rob?"

"Rob is a big boy. He's lived alone for a long time, too. He'll understand that you're doing what you need to do. He'll love you all the more for it."

"But we were going to be married."

"When?"

She had the good grace to lower her head in guilt. "When I felt up to it."

"So you go back to Chester. You get back on your own two feet. You prove to yourself that you're healthy and strong. Then you plan a gorgeous wedding with a maid of honor and bridesmaids and flowers all over the place. Rob won't give you any argument. Take my word for it. Once you've convinced yourself that you're well, you can come to him with the confidence that you're doing so because you want to, not because you need to."

"He said something like that—about wanting rather than needing."

"He's no fool."

"But I've been one."

Albeit apologetically, Jason nodded. Then he took both of her hands in his. "Listen, Heather. I can be blunt with you because you're not really my patient. You don't need a psychiatrist, just a good kick in the pants." They both smiled, he affectionately, she sheepishly. "You're an intelligent, down to earth woman who's been momentarily sidetracked by what, in all fairness, was a very traumatic experience. Now you're going to put it behind you. It's over. Done. You've got a wonderful life ahead of you." He grinned. "Y'know something? I'm damned jealous of old Rob. If you weren't already taken, I'd take you myself. So there!"

After Jason left, Heather cleaned up the kitchen, then went to sit quietly in Rob's den. She thought about the operation and about everything that had happened since. She thought about Rob and about everything he meant to her. She thought about the future and about all she wanted to have.

She knew that Jason's recommendation was a wise one. The thought of going back to Chester alone filled her with dread, but she couldn't argue with his reasons for suggesting it. And she couldn't argue with the fact that she had to do *something*.

She'd been sitting for over an hour, when the phone rang. She was deep in her own thoughts, and it rang a second time before she glanced its way. It could be one of her friends, or Jason, or . . . Rob. She bit her lower lip, then, when the phone rang a third time, slowly reached for it.

"Hello?" she asked softly.

"Heather!" She heard Rob's sigh of relief. "I thought you'd decided not to speak to me anymore."

"No. I was just sitting here thinking."

"Are you all right?"

"I'm fine."

"I . . . I thought I'd come home early. We have to talk. I've been in agony all day."

"I know. Rob?" She took a deep breath. "Would you drive me back to Chester?"

"Is there something you need? I could pick it up."

"No. You've done enough picking up for me. It's time I do that for myself. I want . . . I need to go back there to stay for a while." In the silence that ensued, she heard his unspoken question. "I need to be alone to straighten things out in my mind."

"Things about us? I didn't mean half of what I said this morning, Heather. I love you—"

"I know, and it's not us I have to work out. It's me."

There was another silence. Then, "You haven't lived alone in a long time."

"Neither have you. Are you up for it?"

A third pause. "If you are."

She swallowed, then spoke quietly, but with a confidence she hadn't felt in days. "I'm going to start packing my things. I'll be ready when you get here."

10

HEATHER'S CONFIDENCE began to deteriorate the minute she left Rob's house. It weakened with each mile, and was shaky at best when they pulled up before her house in Chester. By the time Rob left she was a bundle of nerves.

She didn't let him see it, though, and she wouldn't let him phone her. "I'll call you in a few days," she told him, fearing that if she heard from him too soon she'd break down and beg him to come for her.

The first few days were pure torture. She sat in one place, afraid to do much, thinking of Rob, wishing he were there. Any number of scenarios ran through her mind; in each her heart gave out and she was stranded, alone and helpless. She fell asleep that first night only when exhaustion overpowered her hyperactive imagination. To her surprise, she awoke the next morning.

Wary of exerting herself, she didn't do much. She lay in bed for a long time, then, for a change of scenery, settled herself beneath a blanket on the living room sofa. She listened to music, but the lyrics annoyed her, taunted her. She wasn't up for vicarious pleasure.

Time and again she reached for the phone to call Rob. Each time she caught herself and determinedly pulled back her hand.

Rob spent five days in hell before the call finally came. He shot out his hand, then, heart pounding, held it suspended over the receiver. It could be the hospital, he told himself. Or an insurance salesman. No. Too late. It was ten o'clock at night. Was it too late for Heather? Alone, she'd always been in bed by nine. Finally, after the third ring, he picked up the phone.

"Hi, Rob."

He closed his eyes in a moment's prayerful thanks. She sounded wide-awake, stronger, wonderful. "Heather," he breathed. "Hi."

"I . . . I'm not disturbing you, am I?"

"Nah. I was just working. Old habits die hard."

Heather didn't argue. "How have you been?"

He contemplated lying, but couldn't. "Worried as hell wondering how you were."

"But you were in Minneapolis."

"Just for one night, and even then I couldn't stop thinking of you."

"Did you learn what you went to learn?"

"Thoroughly. How are you?"

"I'm fine. Well, better."

"You're feeling okay?"

"Yes."

"What have you done since I dropped you there?"

She contemplated lying, but couldn't. "I spent the first day sitting in a chair staring at the wall. I spent the second day walking around staring at lots of walls. By the third day I could concentrate enough to do a little reading."

He heard her tongue-in-cheek tone. It more than anything said that she was on her way. The fact that she could laugh—well, almost laugh—about herself was a good sign. "And now?"

"I did some sewing today. I spoke with Elaine and I'm working on an order for her. I'll phone the other buyers in another week or two."

"Then you're beginning to feel more confident?"

"Well, I've made it for five days and my heart's still beating. Yes, I'm beginning to feel more confident. I think I needed to do this."

"I think you did, too. But I miss you. It's lonely here. The house is like an empty barn."

"Better an empty barn than one with a bleating sow."

He laughed. "Sows don't bleat. They oink. Ewes bleat."

She grinned. "Whatever." Her grin faded. "I miss you, too, Rob."

"Can I see you?"

"Uh . . . not yet. Not until I'm more sure of myself. It'd be too easy to fall back. . . ." Jason had called her several times and given her the encouragement she'd needed. She felt she was doing the right thing.

"How long do you think it'll take?" Rob asked. With Heather gone, he realized just how much he needed her. But he needed the real Heather, not the one who'd cloaked herself in a robe of insecurity and utter dependence. Even if it killed him—and at times he thought it might—he was willing to wait until that robe had been shed.

"I don't know. I want to get back to work full time, maybe do some other things. I can't give you a time limit, because I don't have one myself." She was doing as Jennifer had suggested. "I do a little more each day than I did the day before. I'm not pushing."

"But you're progressing."

"Yes. I am progressing. Slowly, but steadily."

"Then I'm grateful for that. . . . Can I, uh, will you call me again soon?"

"Uh-huh. Maybe in a day or two."

"I'd like that." His voice softened and broke. "I love you, Heather."

She smiled tearfully. "I love you, too."

IT WAS ACTUALLY three days before Heather called Rob again, but it wasn't for lack of desire. She wanted to have something to say to him, something to make him proud. At last she did.

"I went out driving today."

"You did!"

"Yup. To the supermarket."

"But I thought Sally and Beth were going to keep your refrigerator stocked."

"They were, and they did. But I thought it was about time. I kind of enjoyed it."

"You weren't nervous?"

"Beforehand, you bet. I told myself that if my heart acted up I could collapse against the nearest shelf. Cans or bottles or whatever would topple to the floor, and I'd have instant attention."

"But you didn't collapse."

"No. Halfway through my shopping list, I whipped around the corner of an aisle and crashed into another cart. I terrified a poor little old lady. She told me to slow down. I hadn't realized how fast I was going, and I wasn't even out of breath."

"You've become a menace," he teased, but there was pride in his voice, and she fed off it.

"Maybe. It's a novel experience. Lord only knows what I'll try next."

What she tried was an afternoon at a local ice rink with none other than Jennifer Gibbons, who'd driven up especially for the occasion, wearing outlandish yellow pants and purple leg warmers.

"I think we're both crazy," Jennifer said as they laced on their rented skates.

"You mean, you haven't done this before? You gave me the impression that you were an old hand at it!"

Jennifer shrugged impishly. "Look, it's an indoor rink, so we won't freeze, and there are plenty of gorgeous guys skating around here, just waiting to pick us up if we fall."

"If? That's a laugh. I've never been on skates in my life!"

Jennifer linked her arm with Heather's and tugged her up and off, mumbling under her breath, "That makes two of us . . . but not any moooorrrrrre. . . ."

Heather invited Rob up for dinner the following Sunday. They'd been separated for nearly two weeks, and she was as hungry for the sight of him as he was for her. They held each other tightly at first, then stood back, looked at each other, hugged each other again.

They talked and touched, ate and touched. She showed him the handbags she'd finished and told him about the movie she'd seen the day before with Beth. He told her about the results coming in on a new research project of his and about Helen's new grandchild.

He invited her to spend Christmas Day with him on Long Island with his parents. She accepted.

He knew better than to ask when she'd come back to Woodbridge. Seeing her as she was now, so like the woman he'd fallen in love with, he felt both his heart and his loins swell. He wanted to make love to her, but he wanted her to feel comfortable enough with her own body to want it, really want it, too.

By the time Christmas arrived, Heather was back to putting in a full day's work. She was also venturing out more and more. She'd driven down to see Jennifer in North Branford. She'd even shown up at the hospital one day and dragged a delighted Rob to lunch at the same Greek restaurant he'd taken her to that day she'd had the tests.

She thoroughly enjoyed meeting not only his parents, but his sister and brother and their families, who'd come in for the holidays. On Christmas morning Rob surprised her with a stunning gold pendant, on the back of which were engraved the words, "Always my love. Rob." Heather surprised him with a gold tie tack. Rather than words on the back, there were a series of engraved numbers. When he looked at her in bemusement, she smiled. "Our wedding date . . . assuming you're free. That's two months' notice I'm giving you." He was standing with his mouth open, so she went on. "It'll still be pretty cold here. I was thinking we could go somewhere warm for our honeymoon. Maybe Mexico? I hear there are great ruins to explore."

"Our wedding date," he finally managed to breathe, then beamed. "Our wedding date! I don't believe it!" He raised his fists high in triumph and shouted, "At last!" then lowered his arms around Heather and brought her close. "Come home with me, honey. Tonight. I need you."

She put her arms around his neck and held him tightly. He was hers, the man she adored, and that thought filled her with happiness. She could feel the strength of his body, could smell his familiar scent, could enjoy the pleasurable vibrations shifting through her limbs. But when they made love, she wanted it to be right and good and complete. She wanted to be able to spend the entire night with him, and every one after that.

She still had some growing to do, though, before she could feel strong enough as an individual to come to him that way. Yes, she was back to the schedule she'd kept before the operation. Physically, there was no reason they couldn't make love. They loved each other; they even knew now when they'd be married. But holding off on a return to that physical intimacy was, for Heather, a matter of principle. She wanted to fully prove her independence. She'd given herself two more months. If she reached the point she wanted sooner, she knew she wouldn't stand on ceremony.

"I . . . I want to wait a little longer. Just a little longer, Rob."

He started to argue, then closed his mouth. She was getting there. She was getting there, and he loved her for it.

THEY SAW EACH OTHER every weekend, but Heather balked at seeing Rob during the week. She called him, though, and he called her. It was as though they were courting each other again, but it was different this time. Rather than dreading an eventual operation, Heather was eagerly anticipating a wedding.

At the end of January she did something she'd refused to do in the past. She flew to Washington, D.C., all by herself, to appear at a showing of her handbags at the Neiman-Marcus store there. The week after that, she did another thing she'd refused to do before. She hired a young woman from Hartford, a woman with her own arts and crafts bent, to help out in the less detailed aspects of the production of her bags.

"Atta girl!" Rob exclaimed when she told him. "Now you can keep production at a steady level even while you take time out to travel or honeymoon or...or just spend time with me."

Those had been her thoughts exactly. She hadn't seen the move as one to relieve her of pressure, and she had no intention of apologizing as though that had been the case. It had been an elective, rather than a necessary move.

"Julia is unbelievably skilled. She's been working as a seamstress, tailor-making clothes. She designs a lot of them, and her finished work is impeccable. I wanted to be sure that the quality of the bags remained the same. I think it will."

"If it doesn't, you'll just hire someone else. I'm thrilled you've taken the step.... Are you still planning to go to Boston next week?"

"Uh-huh. Washington went so well that Neiman's wants to do the same thing in the Boston store."

"How long will you be gone?"

"Two days. I thought I'd do a little sight-seeing while I'm there."

"You might get snowed in."

"So I'll bundle up and put on boots."

He cleared his throat. "Pray for snow."

She was confused. "What?"

"I said, 'Pray for snow.' While you're in Boston, I'll be in Vermont . . . skiing."

"Skiing? Rob, I didn't know you skied!"

"I don't. But Gail and Charles are spending a week in the Caribbean and they're leaving the kids with my parents, so I decided to give Mom and Dad a break and take Michael and Dawn skiing for a few days."

"Do they ski?"

"No. We'll all be on the beginner's slope."

Heather smiled. "You're very brave . . . and a wonderful father."

"I'm trying. Gail and Charles had their reservations long before we made our wedding plans. Even though the kids will be coming back East in three weeks for the wedding, they're on school vacation now. I thought it would be kind of nice for me to spend some time alone with them before we're married. I want to let them know how much they do mean to me. . . . You don't mind, do you?"

"Not if you promise to take me with you next time."

"You mean it?"

"Sure. Of course, you may be a whiz on skis by that time. . . ."

It was not to be the case. Heather had returned from Boston and was braiding thongs of leather in her workroom, when the phone rang. Relaxed and thinking pleasant thoughts of Rob and his children on the ski slopes, she set down her work and answered the phone.

"Hello?"

"Heather?"

"Uh-huh?" She frowned and her voice grew cautious. "Dawn?" She'd have recognized the girl's voice even had she not been thinking of her at that moment.

"Yes. I'm sorry to bother you—"

"You're not bothering me. But why aren't you skiing? Is something wrong?"

"Daddy said not call you. He didn't want to disturb you after your trip to Boston and all, but I told him he was being stupid."

"Where are you?"

"In Woodbridge. We got back last night."

"But you were supposed to be skiing for another three days."

"Daddy broke his leg."

Heather sucked in a breath. "He what?"

"He broke his leg."

"Broke his leg? Oh, my God, he didn't!" There was something hilarious about it, though it wasn't funny at all.

"He did. He's in the hospital, and he's been impossible. Really crabby. He's furious that he'll have to slow down and he's convinced that he'll wreck your honeymoon."

Heather wasn't at all worried about that. "Why is he in the hospital? Didn't they set it in Vermont?"

"It was a bad break. He insisted that someone he knew set it. We came down in an ambulance."

"But who's staying with you and Michael?"

"A sitter. Helen's coming for the night, and Daddy's coming home tomorrow morning."

Heather stood quickly. "Listen. I'm going to get some things together and drive down. I'll stay with you and

Michael. In fact, we'll all go out to dinner and then over to the hospital to visit your dad. Sound okay?"

Dawn breathed an audible sigh of relief. Her smile was nearly audible. "I was hoping you'd say that." She lowered her voice to a whisper. "Michael's driving the sitter crazy, and poor Helen will never be able to handle him."

Heather laughed aloud. "I think I can help out. Can you keep the peace until I get there?"

"Sure thing. I'm an expert at handling Michael. A good kick in the shins—"

"Uh, please. Try to restrain yourself, Dawn. We wouldn't want poor Michael to end up with a broken leg, too."

"Then you'd better hurry."

"I'll see you soon."

LEG ENCASED in a white cast and elevated in a sling, Rob was glaring disgruntledly at the television set high on the wall when Dawn and Michael burst into the room with Heather close behind. Michael started talking about the super lasagna they'd had for dinner. Dawn burst into an enthusiastic recounting of Heather's arrival in Woodbridge. Heather stood two feet from the bed with her hands on her hips and broke into her own harangue.

"I can't believe you didn't call me, Robert McCrae! Thank goodness Dawn has some common sense! There I was, sitting up in Chester, happy as a lark because I thought you three were having the time of your lives in Vermont, and here you are with your leg broken in three places, lying alone and in pain in a hospital bed. When were you planning to call me? A day before the wedding? And what were you planning to do in the meantime? It's your right leg. You can't drive. Dawn and Michael will be here for another three days, and you were going to hobble around entertaining them?" She threw her hands in the air. "What do you think I'm for? I'm your fiancée, your almost wife. I'm not helpless or fragile. I can help! I want to help! Do you have any idea how awful I feel—not to mention guilty and angry and hurt?"

Rob was staring at her. So were Dawn and Michael, though the looks on their faces were smug, whereas Rob's was increasingly meek.

"I didn't want to worry you," he finally muttered, his gaze skipping away, then back, almost timidly.

"Didn't want to worry me! My God, Rob. I love you! I want to worry about you. It's my right!"

"Give 'im hell, Heather," Michael said, jabbing at the air with his fist.

Dawn turned on him. "Keep still. This is between Daddy and Heather."

Michael glared. "We were the ones who were with him when it happened."

"Yeah, and if you hadn't yelled to Daddy to slow up, he wouldn't have turned around and gone off the trail into that tree."

Heather had already heard the full story. Three times.

"It wasn't my fault," Michael returned, scowling. "Heather said it wasn't."

"But why don't you learn for once to keep your big mouth shut?"

Heather went to stand between brother and sister, putting an arm around each pair of shoulders. "Look, you two, I think maybe I should bawl your father out in private. His ego may not be able to take too much of this public stuff. How about you both go down to the coffee shop and get some dessert." She reached into her bag and put a five-dollar bill in Michael's hand. "You keep track of the money, Michael. Dawn, you keep track of the time. Twenty minutes. If you're not back by then, I'll send out the Mounties."

The children started for the door. "That might be fun— a run-in with the Mounties," Michael remarked.

Dawn eyed him in despair. "There aren't any Mounties here, stupid. She was teasing."

Michael wasn't to be outdone. "Watch it, smart lips, or I won't give you money for a sundae. As a matter of fact, you don't need a sundae. Zits . . . remember?"

The last thing Heather and Rob saw was Dawn taking a swipe at Michael's head before the two disappeared into the hall.

Heather waited, listening. "No shrieks. I guess they've settled it."

"Heather?" Rob was grasping for her hand, his voice sounding hoarse. She turned to find him looking at her so soulfully that her heart nearly broke. His face was pale and drawn. There were dark smudges beneath his eyes, and his hair was mussed. "I didn't mean to make you angry, or hurt you by not calling you. I was upset and uncomfortable and embarrassed. Here I thought I was doing such a nice thing with my children, and we were really having a good time of it that first day, and then I went and blew it all."

"You didn't blow it all," she said softly. The interlude with Dawn and Michael had reduced her anger to nil. Or maybe it had been Rob's heartrending expression. Or the fact that they were alone and that for a change, he was the one truly in need.

She carefully eased herself onto the bed by his hip and closed her hands around his. "Don't you see? It doesn't really matter what you do with Michael and Dawn, as long as you do something. They don't think any less of you for what happened, and I'm sure if it's handled right they'll have a fun time nursing you."

"What about you? I don't want to be a burden."

"Burden? What burden?" She grinned and looked at his casted leg. "It's a little refreshing to have the tables turned. How does it feel to be a patient, doctor?"

"It sucks," he grumbled.

"Uh-uh, none of that language."

"Well, it does. A fine groom I'll make hobbling down the aisle. And our honeymoon—I'll be the sight to see when we show up at the ruins."

"You might at that. I guess I'll have to call the travel agent and change the reservations. I hear there are a couple of places on Antigua that are beautiful and quiet. Nothing to do but eat late breakfasts and sumptuous dinners and lie in the sun and read."

"That'll be boring as hell for you."

"It'll be nice and restful. I may need it after chauffeuring you around for the next three weeks."

"You don't have to—"

"I want to." She framed his face in her hands and leaned close. As uncharacteristically disheveled as he looked, she adored everything about him. "I love you, Rob. It doesn't matter where we go or what we do. If we don't traipse through ruins this time, we'll do it another time. It'll be something to look forward to. The important thing, the most important thing, the only thing that matters is that we're together.... Yes?"

His eyes grew suspiciously moist. Wrapping his arms around her, he pulled her head to his chest. "Oh . . . yes...."

ROB WAS IN SHEER AGONY, but it was the most delightful agony he'd ever known. His eyes were closed, his body strained upward. His fingers wound tightly through Heather's hair, and he was breathing hard.

"Heather . . . my God . . . oh, sweet...."

When she felt he was nearing his peak, she slid up over him, thighs straddling his hips, and impaled herself upon that part of him she'd been loving so eloquently with her lips and tongue. She sighed in pleasure, then gasped when he arched more deeply into her. He filled her fully, physically and emotionally. She could never imagine it any other way.

Hands braced by his shoulders, she looked into his eyes as she slowly raised, then lowered her hips. "I love you," she mouthed, saw the vow returned, then closed her eyes, arched her back and concentrated on the wealth of sensation radiating from the point of their physical union and from their hearts.

He raised his head, took her nipple into his mouth and drew on it. When she began to moan and move faster, he gave her other breast similar attention. Then he ran his tongue along the fading pink line bisecting her chest, drinking the heat-induced moisture from her skin until he, too, was swept up in the rhythm she set and together they reached a throbbing climax.

Physically satiated and exquisitely happy, Heather finally eased down to his side, leaving one leg resting between his bare one and the one in its cast. When he caught her hand and brought it to his damp chest, their wedding bands clicked softly together. They didn't speak, simply enjoyed the aftermath of loving. And the peace of the Antigua night. And the knowledge that forever lay rich and promising ahead.